Paul -
Enjoy the next phase
of your life's
journey.
　　　Sincerely,
　　　　Your colleagues
　　　on the orange &
　　　Silver teams.

Laurie Erickson

Steve Blacker

Jo Gibson

Grace Oliphart

Paul, it was wonderful to
work with you. You
are a fine man and
deserve great happiness.
Enjoy + relax. Cordially,

Paul:
Have the special!
with sausage, scrambled
and Rye toast! Let's keep
in touch. We will miss you
Jim Balshaw

Lessons on the Journey

Lessons on the Journey

SHORT STORIES BY

David Nimmer

NODIN PRESS
Minneapolis

ISBN: 0-931714-72-9

Nodin Press, a division of Micawber's, Inc.
525 North Third Street
Minneapolis, MN 55401

Contents

· ·

v

CONTENTS

Foreword

. . . .

When I was a boy growing up, I was always small for my age—the runt of the litter, as one veteran Minneapolis homicide cop would later graphically put it. Being small and looking boyish meant I had to struggle a little harder for acceptance in the world of men.

In the army, I couldn't find a pair of fatigues that fit. In college, I couldn't find a bar where they wouldn't ask for identification. And in the newsroom of The Minneapolis Star, I didn't last a week before one of the veteran reporters mistook me for a copy boy.

During the three-and-a-half decades that have passed since then, it's been my life's adventure to make sense of all the rituals, traditions, expectations and exhortations that get passed along from father to son, big brother to little brother, best friend to best friend, platoon sergeant to buck private, wife to husband. I'm now more aware than ever that my life has been shaped by the quest to find out what a good man is and how he's supposed to behave.

These stories reflect the lessons on that journey: some painful, some hopeful and a few, I believe, even insightful. There's at least a grain of truth from my own life and times in each of them. But the grains are too few, the threads too thin, for these stories to be true representations from my life. They are, however, a part of real life—the real life of almost everyone I've met, twenty-two or eighty-two.

I hope that readers of this volume, especially those who shared part of my journey, resist the urge to put names, faces and real places to these stories. They are fiction, albeit an embroidery of real threads and fabric. To the friends and family who've supplied the cloth, I give my thanks and love. To those who've caused discomfort, the effects were only temporary and the blame half mine.

I owe a special debt to Norton Stillman, who published this book as well as my first; to J.B. Sisson, who wielded an insistent but graceful editing pencil; to Tom Connery, my University of St. Thomas department chair, who offered support and encouragement; and to Kris, my wife, whose love and honesty cast a revealing light on my search for manly virtues—which turn out to be, after all, human virtues.

Lessons on the Journey

We're Men, Aren't We?

. . . .

JAKE WAS holding onto the bow of the eighteen-foot Old Town canoe, helping me balance it on my hip.

"Now, put your right hand across your left and grab the yoke," he said. "Then it's just a nice, smooth motion up onto your shoulders."

I pulled up with my arms, rolled my shoulders, and tried to swing under the canoe. I lost my grip, and the canoe clattered to the ground.

"God, Jake," I muttered, "I'm sorry. I just don't know whether I've got enough upper body strength to hoist the damned thing."

It was a poor time to find out we had a problem. We had set up our camp for the night at the public landing at Crane Lake, and the next morning the outfitter's boat would take us to the Bottle River portage. There we would begin our five-day trip into the Quetico-Superior wilderness.

Jake effortlessly swung the canoe onto his shoulders. I'd felt uneasy about this canoe trip ever since Jake proposed it six months ago, since I hadn't been camping in ten years.

We'd worked together for years, and I'd liked Jake from the start. He had an energetic, bigger-than-life approach to damned near everything he did. When he cooked, it was a filet gumbo with fresh shrimp and okra. When he hammered and sawed, it was a three-shelf bookcase with sliding doors. When he pitched, it was seven shut-out innings at the company softball game. I had been given to bouts of hero worship since second grade whenever someone could run faster, jump higher, punch harder, or yell louder. Jake never asked for such deference, but I kept wanting to measure up. The rivalry had become more intense since I hadn't seen much of Jake for the past four years, after he'd taken another job at an office across town.

He was still snoring softly when I awakened from a restless sleep with a mosquito swelling with blood from the back of my hand. I shook her off, quietly unzipped the tent flap, and emptied my bladder at the base of a birch tree. It was going to be a gray day, I figured, a bit on the cool side for mid-August. I was still gazing at the dock down the bay from the Crane Lake campground when I heard Jake stir.

"We'd better haul ass," he said. "The outfitter's going to meet us in a half hour, and we've got to get the canoe and packs over there."

We folded the tent, rolled up the sleeping bags, and stuffed all that nylon and down into the tiniest of bags. It was all Jake's gear.

We threw three fully loaded Duluth packs into the outfitter's runabout and put the canoe on the boat's pipe rack. The pilot, a twenty-year-old college student named Ben, looked at the size of the packs and smiled.

He turned the key, the seventy-five horsepower Mercury rumbled to life, and we left the dock with a roar. Fifteen minutes later we were snaking up the Loon River around stumps, logs, and rocks in the deep, dark water. I could almost touch the trees on either shore.

We coasted in to a rickety wooden dock beside a small waterfall. Ben tied the boat to the dock, and a railroad flatcar crawled over the top of a hill and slid down into the water. Ben eased the boat into the cradle of the flatcar and waved his arm. With a loud chugging of the mechanical lift's diesel engine, the car carried us up and over to the other side, to Lac LaCroix.

Once on the big lake, Ben hit the throttle, and the runabout jumped up on plane. We skimmed along for the next half hour, flying past the Indian village, the fancy fishing lodge for rich tourists, and the ranger station on Hilly Island. Then Ben eased the bow into a narrow bay and cut the throttle.

"I'm going to let you out here," he said. "Too many rocks to get in any closer."

He helped Jake put the canoe in the water and handed him the packs. I climbed into the canoe's stern seat and picked up the paddle.

"Just head for that little waterfall over there," Ben said. "I'll see you here in five days, one hour either side of noon."

It was only a hundred yards to the portage trailhead, next to a creek that tumbled out of the brush. We slid the canoe onto the pebble shoreline and unloaded the packs.

"I'll carry the canoe and one of the packs," Jake said, "and we'll come back for the third one and anything else we left behind. Put your pack on that fallen tree limb and ease into the shoulder straps and stand up. That's a lot easier than trying to jerk those seventy pounds off the ground onto your back."

He held the pack while I slid into the straps and tightened them. Then I tried to stand up. I staggered, almost fell over backward, and managed to steady myself.

"You going to be all right?" Jake asked.

"Hell, yeah," I shot back.

He lifted the canoe up onto his shoulders and started off down the boulder-strewn path. I followed, staggering but managing to move my feet fast enough to keep from falling on my face. For the first two hundred yards the footing was solid, but then the path disappeared into a pool of black, sticky mud. The brush was so thick I couldn't leave the narrow path. I leaned forward and put one foot in front of the other, holding onto the small popple trees for support. Mud oozed over the tops of my brand-new Gortex boots. The pack straps dug into my shoulders. Streaks of sweat ran down my glasses and stung my eyes. My breath was coming in gasps that burned my lungs. My heart was beating in a staccato rhythm under my sweat-soaked shirt. Then I slipped and fell.

I landed on my back on top of the pack. I could feel the mud on my neck. I couldn't get on my feet. What the hell was I doing out here in the first place? Why

hadn't I stopped smoking at twenty instead of forty? What was Jake going to think of me: some wimp who couldn't even carry a pack without falling on his ass? And how was I ever going to make it through five days?

For a moment I stopped thrashing and lay still. God, just let me get a frigging grip on this. I took a deep breath and rolled on my side by a small birch tree. I reached up as high as I could and grabbed the trunk. I was up on my knees when the pack shifted, yanked on my shoulders, and tumbled me back into the mud bath. I tried again, and this time I got to my feet. For a minute or so, I just stood there, regaining my balance.

After tightening the pack straps, I leaned forward and started to walk. As the trail wound uphill, the ground was drier, and I walked faster. The pack was more comfortable, and I felt more sure-footed. I began to think of the mud on my face, shirt, hands, pack, everywhere, as a merit badge. "Just keep walkin'," I told myself, "that's all you've got to do."

By the time I spotted the canoe on the shore of Crooked Lake, Jake was coming back up the trail.

"Oh shit," he said. "That was a gut-busting portage. How are you doing?"

I told him I had become intimately acquainted with Mother Earth a quarter of a mile back, and he laughed. Together we walked back for the rest of the gear. This trip was a walk in the park compared to the first.

In the canoe again, we headed for Rebecca Falls, twin cascades of water around a granite island. Jake had heard the island was full of blueberries, and we found thousands of small bushes laden with berries, tiny, sweet—real blueberries. It took fifteen minutes to get a handful, and the best berries were on the bushes just above the cascading falls, where the mist settled on the leaves. We picked enough for a taste and had a sockful left over for supper.

By the time we found a campsite, two portages away on the Siobhan River, we were well past hungry— we were famished. We pitched the tent, rolled out the sleeping bags, and unpacked the cook gear. I was dog tired, and every muscle above my waist cried out for mercy, but I never felt better. Jake baked blueberry biscuits. We ate red beans and rice and raw-fried potatoes and washed it all down with strong black coffee. After I washed the dishes, I sat on a log and watched the sun slip toward the horizon. There was no breeze or sound or bug. The pines on the far bank of the river were enveloped with the soft gold of sunset. A pair of mink frolicked on the rock in front of us, as if they knew we bore them no harm.

Jake and I hadn't said a word for more than an hour, when he lit a smudge of sage and piñon pine. For the past few months I'd been listening to his tape of the words of Black Elk describing Indian rituals. We let the sweet smoke waft over us. We talked about our fathers, both in nursing homes, and how they would have enjoyed the woods and water. We talked until the light was gone, and we slept the sleep of the carefree and the exhausted.

For the next two days under cloudless skies we paddled and portaged. The portages seemed to get easier. Jake could sling the canoe onto his shoulders and step off at a brisk pace. I could hoist the pack to my back and almost trot down the trail. My heart no longer raced, and I no longer gasped for breath. Jake's map reading and navigating were flawless, and we never missed a portage trailhead. On one of the portages through a pine and popple forest we discovered a creek that dropped from pool to pool, and we stripped off our jeans and T-shirts and sat in the middle of the stream, and the cool water washed away sweat and grime and wrinkled our skin. For several hours we searched for the Indian pictographs at Darky Lake and were ready to give up when Jake spied a splash of color at the base of a granite cliff. We paddled closer, and there they were: tiny, rust-colored figures of man and moose and moose horns. Each tine on each rack of the moose was painted clearly and crisply. We floated in front of them, enchanted by their delicacy and permanence.

That night we camped on an island about half a mile away. In the middle of a small fire pit we discovered a faint penciled note that warned of a rogue bear wandering the island, scaring at least one camper. We filled our bellies with chicken stew, stowed our food pack high in a tree, and threw a couple of extra birch logs on the fire. The bear stayed away.

The next morning we had coffee and pancakes and slices of thick slab bacon, which I never ate at home.

Jake said we'd need plenty of fuel to paddle the Darky River, a river of different moods and plenty of portages.

At first the Darky looked hospitable. The banks were lined with overhanging cedars, the current was gentle, and the water was deep and free of rocks and logs. The rhythm of our paddling was almost effortless. I paused to watch an eagle soaring overhead, catching the air currents, and perching on a dead limb atop a white pine.

"Watch out!" Jake hollered. "On your right!"

I dug the paddle into the water, but it was too late. We slid right into the middle of a logjam, huge floating tree trunks and limbs. Jake tried to back us out, but the current was too strong, and we had no room to maneuver. As the logs bumped against the sides of the canoe, we spun around. The bow was now pointed upstream, and Jake was clutching a branch.

"I'm going to try and get out," he said. "Maybe I can walk on top of this jam and pull us around."

I grabbed a log to steady the canoe while Jake climbed out. He managed to stand for a moment, but the logs rolled, and he fell. His left foot was wedged between the canoe and the timber.

"Hold on," I yelled. "I'm getting out."

I clambered over the gunwale and tried to kneel on a big pine log still covered with bark. It was slippery, and I slid off into the cold, dark water between the branches. I kicked my feet but couldn't feel the bottom.

"You all right?" Jake shouted.

I kicked my feet again and my body popped up enough for me to swing an arm around the tree trunk.

"Yeah," I hollered back. "I got my head out from under now."

But how could we get out of here without dumping the canoe? By now Jake had found a steady log to stand on, and he was slowly pulling the canoe toward him. I let go of the tree and grabbed the canoe and looked up.

"Nothing to worry about, old buddy," Jake said from above. "We're men, aren't we?"

I pulled myself along the gunwale to where Jake was kneeling and clambered up beside him on a little log raft with solid footing. We looked like drowned rats. Jake's dark glasses were on top of his head. His sleeve was torn. My knuckles were scraped. My wallet was soaked. We looked at each other and laughed until tears came to our eyes and our sides ached. We re-arranged the packs and eased the canoe to the other side of our log raft. The water was clear ahead, and we climbed in and began to paddle.

The rest of the day was uneventful except for half a dozen uphill portages around logjams and rapids. The longest was a quarter of a mile and the path was narrow and full of boulders. I pulled one of the ligaments in my lower back when I picked up the food pack. It was a sharp stab that sucked the breath out of my chest. I lurched forward and climbed to the top of the bank. This portage took half an hour.

By the time I got to the other side, Jake was fishing, up to his knees at the edge of the roils and waves of the rapids. We both loved to fish but had decided this wouldn't be a fishing trip—all we wanted now was supper. I used a spinning rod and a small crank bait, casting to an eddy at the edge of the rapids. I looked up and saw Jake's pole bent, almost doubled over.

"Fish?" I hollered.

"Gumbo."

The smallmouth broke water with a roll. She was fat and feisty. Jake put her on a rope stringer, and we fished for another fifteen minutes, catching and releasing three or four stocky smallmouth. One fish, four pounds or more, was enough.

That evening, Jake's fish gumbo was hot and spicy and gut-filling. I ate three bowls, and the last one brought out a sweat on my brow. As usual, I collapsed after dark and awakened only when I heard Jake cursing at the balky propane stove.

This was our last day, through Minn Lake, part of McAree, and then back into Lac LaCroix. The wind was up by the time we broke camp, and it was a tough paddle into the whitecaps rolling across the water. My lower back was giving me fits. When we got to the portage into McAree, Jake said he'd carry all the packs. I protested.

"Look," he advised, "let me help you out. You've done your part."

I carried the rods and a few odds and ends, and Jake lugged the rest. I paddled hard, though, and we could still move the canoe at a brisk pace. It began to rain, and the temperature dropped about fifteen degrees.

We pulled on our ponchos and kept paddling. We caught a few smallmouth at Brewer Rapids and cut some firewood on McAree.

By late afternoon the skies were clearing as we reached Hilly Island, near our pickup spot. As we pitched camp, Jake looked tired, and I felt sore. I was famished. Jake made chili and corn bread, while I unrolled our sleeping bags and swept out the tent. We were back in civilization now: the campsite had a picnic table. I wolfed down a bowl of chili and was about to get another, when I saw Jake lying on the ground, exhausted, asleep with an arm tucked under his head. He still had a spoon in his hand. I got a sleeping bag from the tent, draped it over him, and took the spoon from his fingers.

When I went back to my chili and corn bread, I noticed on the table a little memo pad, Jake's journal. I couldn't resist a look at the last few pages.

"It was a fitting way to finish the trip," he had written. "We've paddled seventy-five miles, read the ancient vermilion stories on the cliff walls, taken a dunk in a logjam, eaten some proper meals, and been quiet a lot. We pitched camps on slick rocks that we shared with moose and mink. We offered tobacco, and gifts came back to us. And for the campfires and friendship and memories, I thank you."

I closed the notebook and picked up my coffee cup. Damn, I thought, what a strange kind of creature we are, we men. On this night, at least, I was content to let it be a mystery. But I sure did want a heating pad.

A Man Going Around Taking Names

. . . .

$\mathcal{H}$ANK HUNG UP the phone, pushed the chair back, and propped his feet up on the rolltop desk in his tiny den. The call had been bad news, and it brought back a headful of memories about his old friend. He hadn't seen Willie in almost four years. In the meantime Hank had got married, changed jobs, and bought a house in the country.

Hank's memories took him back fifteen years to the frigid February morning when he and Willie met. Hank, then a very young reporter for a city magazine, was struggling with a story about black entrepreneurs in the Twin Cities. Willie had just opened a small car wash in south Minneapolis, promising motorists a chance to "get rid of winter's overcoat and see the car underneath." When Hank walked into the office beside the washing bay, the warm, moist air fogged his glasses, and as he groped for the desk in front of him, he was startled by a gruff and raspy voice: "Looking for someone, peepsight?" Hank smiled. He hadn't heard that phrase since basic training, from a crusty platoon sergeant referring to his recruits who wore glasses.

They shook hands, and Willie fired up one of the sixty Salem cigarettes he smoked every day. For the next two hours Willie told the story of how after the Watts riot he moved from Los Angeles to the Twin Cities, leaving his nearly grown kids behind. "But what the hell," he said, "I had to do something with my life, and there was nothing left for me back there." For two years he worked as a night janitor in a Minneapolis office building, while trying to shake loose some money from the Small Business Administration to open a car wash. "I know something about cleaning up after people. If you're born black and poor, peepsight, you learn how to clean up after the man. If I can make a buck washing his wheels," he concluded, "then I'll take his green and do it with a smile." Willie bought the car wash with twenty thousand dollars down from the SBA and struggled to break even, open six days a week from seven in the morning until eight at night. Willie, probably in his fifties, was working thirteen hours a day, soaping up cars, wiping them off, offering a kick in the ass to one or another of the dozen kids who worked for him. In Hank's article Willie was mentioned prominently and featured in the photograph.

Now Hank stared at the phone number on his desk. Willie's son had called to say that his father was dying of prostate cancer. The number was for Willie's new suite in a fancy suburban office building. Hank started to dial the number but stopped just before the last digit. He was gripped by fear, guilt, and remorse.

They'd been such good friends, the big black man and the little white boy. Willie had seen most of the world, drunk a good share of its Scotch whiskey, heard a lot of its blues, and tasted enough of its pleasures and pains to know the difference, and Willie was a damned good teacher. For a decade the two drank together, traveled together, and survived together, survived bad times and good, divorces and second marriages, a foreclosure and more than one grand opening.

Maybe it was the successes, Hank thought, that caused the two to drift apart. As Willie's business flourished and he opened his third car wash, their conversations became awkward and painful and laughter seemed harder to come by. For Hank the final straw had been a phone call from Willie.

"You know," Willie had said, "the trouble with you—"

"Willie, the trouble with me is that I'm tired of listening to you talking about the trouble with me."

But now Willie was dying. The next morning Hank phoned him at his office.

"Willie," he said, "this is Hank. I'd like to see you."

"Peepsight," he said in a subdued voice, "long time, no see. I've been under the weather, and I'm only coming in for an hour a day. Let's make it tomorrow, about nine."

At quarter to nine Hank pulled up in front of the three-story glass and steel aquarium that housed a hundred accountants, lawyers, financial advisers, and business executives—a long way from the damp office in Willie's first car wash. On the third floor in the suite at the end of the hall, where Midwest Auto Detailing was engraved in black and gold on the door, a cheerful secretary said that Willie hadn't arrived yet but had left instructions for Hank to make himself at home in Willie's office.

The office was huge, with a desk of glass and chrome and chairs of black leather, big and soft. The walls were covered with photographs of Willie opening a new car wash, Willie at a New York convention, Willie shaking hands with the mayor. There was

nothing modest about this office, Hank noted, and that was entirely in character for Willie—a hustler, a promoter—and this drive helped him battle the odds and keep going through his twelve-hour workdays. Looking around the office, Hank suddenly felt very proud of his old friend.

After waiting awhile Hank wandered down the hallway, past a conference room, a tiny kitchen, and a large storage room with boxes of detergents, waxes, and polishing cloths stacked to the ceiling. Painted on the far wall of this room was a large grey gravestone with the letters "R.I.P." Underneath, there were three rows of names in bold black letters. A legend over the gravestone read, "Here Lie the Bodies of Those Who Tried to Fuck with Willie Smith." Midway down the first column was Hank's name.

Hank felt the gall of anger well up in his throat. He slumped into a chair. What would cause a man to hire a painter to put the names of his enemies on the wall? There were a dozen more questions and no answers that Hank could find satisfactory, save for one. Anger had always been the fuel Willie used to keep on battling. And Hank had to admit that he was the one who had ended their friendship.

Hank was still in the chair when the secretary came and beckoned him to Willie's office. Willie was sitting behind his desk, holding an unlit cigarette and wearing a sailor's cap. Willie liked to dress well, but the crisp lines of his white shirt and grey slacks couldn't hide the loose skin and the sharp angles of his shoulders and elbows. He'd lost fifty or sixty pounds, and he seemed to have difficulty holding his head up.

"So how are you doing?" Willie murmured almost inaudibly.

"Okay, and how are you feeling?"

"I'm a little under the weather, peepsight, but it's

only temporary. The bastards aren't going to be able to get me down. I've got a couple more chemotherapy treatments, and the sawbones says I can beat this thing."

"You're looking pretty good," Hank lied. "Besides, only the good die young. You've got at least fifty more years."

Willie cracked a half-hearted smile, and they talked about mutual friends and the car-washing business.

"Willie," Hank said after an awkward pause, "I want to tell you some things, and this ain't easy, so just hear me out. First, I love you. You taught me some good things and showed me some great sights. I'm grateful. Two, I'm sorry that we split, and I don't think either of us should take the blame." Shit, Hank thought, this is beginning to sound like a speech. But it was the only way he knew how to say it. "I want to remember the good times—the trips and the music and all the stories. And last, I'd like you to take me off your wall. I saw it in the other room. And I don't think my name belongs there."

Willie was looking down at his empty desktop. He waved his hand feebly in front of his face.

"It's been nice to see you, peepsight," he said. "But I'm getting kind of tired. This chemo knocks the shit out of me. Thanks for coming."

Hank stood up and shook Willie's hand. It felt cold and lifeless.

"Thanks for hearing me out," Hank said. "I'll say a prayer for you, big fella."

As he drove away, Hank couldn't shake the empty feeling, the space where the pieces didn't fit together anymore.

A month later Hank heard that Willie had died, surrounded by his wife and three of his kids in a suburban hospital. When the newspaper's obituary editor phoned, Hank told her about Willie's hard work, gritty perseverance, and old-fashioned courage. The next day the paper ran a color photo of Willie on the front page, keying it to the obituary in the metro section. Hank went to the memorial service, paid his respects to the family, and soon was immersed again in his busy daily life.

In the following February, Hank found himself at Willie's office building when he interviewed a lawyer for an article about the civil litigation clogging the dockets of county courts. After the interview Hank looked in on the offices of Midwest Auto Detailing. He'd heard that Willie's son was running the business now, and he asked for him. In her same cheerful manner the secretary said he wasn't in.

"I just wondered," Hank said, "whether I could take one more look at Willie's office?"

With a wave of her hand she told him to go ahead. Hank went directly to the storage room. The wall was blank: the gravestone with the columns of names had been covered with a coat of high-gloss ivory paint. On his way out, Hank stopped at the secretary's desk.

"I was just noticing," he said, "that Willie's list is gone from the wall."

"Oh yes," she said, with a smile. "Willie called from the hospital the week before he died. He told me to 'get the goddamned wall painted.'"

Out in the parking lot Hank looked at the streaks of salt and slush on his old blue Chev. It was time, he decided, to get the car washed.

The Affair

. . . .

*G*REG ROLLED over and put his head on the pillow, his heart still racing and his hair damp from making love. Cindy, his wife, lay next to him. He could hear her breathing. Neither said a word.

In the past, their lovemaking had a passion, an intensity, even a sense of adventure. Some of that had waned in the last three years, because of familiarity and opportunity, Greg assumed. But this time was different: it was as though Cindy weren't there. It was like painting by numbers. And he didn't know what to say or do about it.

But he thought he knew what was going on: Cindy was having an affair with a guy they both worked with. Greg and Cindy had met at a Saint Paul ad agency. He was an account executive, and she was a copywriter just out of college. He'd noticed her the first day she came to work, asked her out the first week and married her a year later. Bill had started as a copywriter a month after Cindy did. They quickly became friends. They were both rookies, they were both ambitious, and they both loved folk-rock and expensive restaurants. Greg was eight years older than they were, and at first he paid little attention to their friendship.

Besides, Greg had his share of good women friends, two in particular, with whom he shared dinners and secrets. He wanted his wife to have the same freedom, but in the last six weeks he had been watching Cindy and Bill at work. He thought he'd detected a growing intimacy between them—glances, touches on the shoulder, smiles that lingered too long. For days now, he'd actively pushed the thoughts from his consciousness.

Tonight in bed, though, they were there to stay. He listened to the regular rhythm of Cindy's breathing. She's screwing another guy, he thought, and here she is sound asleep. He was gritting his teeth. He got up and drank a glass water. He decided he had to know for sure.

At the breakfast table the next morning Greg set his little trap. He poured his second cup of coffee and looked up at Cindy, who was fiddling with her hair and reading the morning paper, and said, "Babe, I'm going to take a fishing trip next weekend, if it's all right with you, to Lake of the Woods. One of the guys in our soft-ball league got a special deal, and the walleye fishing has been hot."

"That's great," she said, looking up. "How long are you going to be gone?"

"I'll leave after work Friday and be back late Sunday night, about nine or ten."

During the next week Greg and Cindy didn't talk much and didn't touch except for a perfunctory goodnight kiss. But each night Greg set out another piece of equipment—rain suit, rods and reels, tackle box. Friday after work, he rushed home, showered, and changed into a flannel shirt and jeans. Cindy was already home, as Greg suspected she would be.

"You guys have a long way to drive, and it gets dark early now," she said. "You better be on your way."

Greg gave her a hug, kissed her on the cheek, and hauled his fishing gear out to his Bronco. He parked a block behind Cindy's powder-blue Camaro and waited in the dusk.

Fifteen minutes later, carrying an overnight bag and wearing jeans, a blue work shirt, and her hair in a pony-tail, Cindy came out the front door of their apartment complex. She headed north on Snelling Avenue, and he followed her out onto the highway toward Duluth. The two cars settled into a comfortable pace at sixty-five miles an hour, but Greg was growing uneasy. He hadn't thought about what he was going to do when Cindy met up with Bill. Would he burst into their motel room? Would he follow them around for the weekend? Would he stop them on the street? What would he say? Now he realized he didn't want to see Cindy with Bill. This was the woman he fell in love with, the woman he promised God he would honor and cherish for the rest of his life. He cringed at the thought of her holding hands or kissing or making love to that blond, blue-eyed son of a bitch. Bill was half a foot taller and fifty pounds heavier than Greg. He couldn't even beat him up.

The Camaro was almost out of sight, and Greg

suddenly turned off at the Pine City exit. He pulled up at the Red Shed Cafe and ordered a cheeseburger and coffee. His hands were shaking. He ate half of the cheeseburger, drained the coffee cup quickly and headed back to St. Paul.

When he walked into the apartment, he stumbled over the ironing board in the dark kitchen. Cindy must have been ironing a blouse or dress. He wondered whether Bill had a favorite outfit he liked her to wear. Greg lit a filter-tip Kool, turned on *The Tonight Show*, and stared at the screen. He was still in front of it at two o'clock. That weekend he smoked so many cigarettes and drank so much coffee that the sound of a car horn on the street would jolt him from the chair at the kitchen table.

By Sunday night he was in an angry frenzy. *Sixty Minutes* had just finished when Greg heard the key in the door. Cindy walked in with her overnight bag.

"Oh, you're home," she said, smiling. "How was the fishing?"

"It looks like you've been traveling. Where have you been?"

Cindy brushed past him and threw her bag on their bed. "Well," she said, "it was such a nice fall day on Saturday that I decided to drive down along the river and look at the leaves."

"Stop this bullshit! You didn't drive south. You drove north, and you left on Friday night. I followed you, goddammit." He took Cindy by the arm and gently led her to the couch in the living room. He knelt in front of

26

her. "All right," he said, "I want the truth. I know you were with Bill. I've suspected this for a long time." He stood up. She looked contrite. She seemed so tiny, so delicate, he didn't know whether he wanted to hug her or hit her.

She sighed. "I guess you're entitled to the truth," she said, so softly he could hardly hear. "I was with Bill this weekend on the North Shore. I only slept with him a couple of times. We were friends. And it got out of hand."

"No, it's not out of hand," Greg said. "You put our lives, my life, out of control."

Tears were streaming down Cindy's face. For a minute or two she couldn't talk, couldn't catch her breath. "I didn't mean to hurt you," she mumbled with a sob. "I didn't mean for it to happen. I love you."

Greg knelt in front of her again. "What about him?" he said. "Do you love him too?"

She started to answer and then paused. Greg felt he might vomit. He could taste the acid in the back of his throat.

"I don't know," she said. "I just don't know."

This is insane, Greg thought. She loves me. She doesn't know whether she loves him. She's sleeping with me, she's screwing him. We all work in the same office, and we're all supposed to be at work at nine tomorrow morning.

"I don't know what we're going to do, babe," he said. "I don't have a clue."

They didn't talk much for the rest of the evening,

and in bed that night Greg lay for about five minutes, inhaling the faint musky scent of her perfume. He'd always liked it. Bill probably liked it too. He sat up.

"I can't be in the same bed with you," he said. "The thought of him next to you last night—it makes me crazy."

He put on his robe, went out to the living room, lit a Kool, and watched the sun come up. Cindy was still asleep when he left for work. She called in sick and stayed home.

Bill was there, though, and Greg could see him from his office cubicle. He was wearing a blue-striped shirt with a white collar, a light blue tie, suspenders, and a pair of maroon penny-loafers. He was well-built, with broad shoulders and a boyish face. Everything about him looked styled, combed, pressed, and self-possessed. Greg wanted to smash him in the mouth, to watch a trickle of blood run onto that designer shirt. He went to the men's room and looked in the mirror. There were circles under his eyes, the collar on his blue shirt was frayed, and cigarette smoke had stained his teeth. He smiled at this image in the mirror, though.

Greg didn't speak to Bill that day. He had to walk past his desk several times, but he avoided eye contact. Bill seemed to be having a good day, chatting with the secretaries, phoning clients, reading some of his copy to colleagues. Greg worried that someone in the office might find out what was going on. Maybe everybody already knew he was a cuckold, to be pitied and whispered about in the lunchroom. At three o'clock he went home.

Cindy wanted to talk. They sat together on the couch, and she said she'd been thinking about what happened and why. "Maybe I was too young when we got married," she said. "Maybe I just wanted an adventure. Whatever it is, I know I love you and I want our marriage to last."

Greg started to cry. "I love you, too," he said, taking off his glasses and wiping his eyes with the back of his hand. "I expected this marriage to last for the rest of my life. I wanted to have kids. I wanted to grow old with you. I still want that. But I don't know whether I can trust you, not the way I did."

She took him in her arms and stroked the back of his head. She promised not to see Bill again except at the office. She would break off the relationship and explain to Bill that her marriage was too important. "You're going to have to trust me, Greg," she said. "I can do this. This is what I want."

He held her face in his hands. "You got the hard part up front, babe," he said, "and that's the trusting part. I'm going to try. I can do the forgiveness. It's the forgetting that's hard."

For the next two days they both went to work. Greg finished an ad campaign for a grocery chain. Cindy wrote a magazine ad for a bridal shop, and the client raved over it. Bill was out of the office at a workshop. On Wednesday night Greg and Cindy went out to dinner at their favorite restaurant along the river and ate giant prawns in ginger sauce. They talked about spending a long weekend up north, maybe to a bed and breakfast near Ely.

The next morning when Cindy got up, Greg said he was sleeping in because he had a night meeting with a client and wouldn't be home until late. By the time he got to work, Cindy was out at a day-long meeting at a video-production house, so he never had a chance to tell her that his client had canceled their meeting for that night. He got home at six-thirty and found the apartment empty.

He waited for half an hour and then drove down Fairview Avenue past Bill's apartment building. He'd been there at parties a couple of times. He was relieved when he didn't see Cindy's Camaro. He continued south for another block and turned onto Jefferson. Then he saw it, the Camaro, the fourth car from the corner. She'd parked two and a half blocks away.

He returned down the alley and pulled up in back of Bill's building. His apartment, at the rear, was dark. He felt his pulse quicken and put the car in gear. The last thing he wanted was for some cop squad to roll through the alley and think they had found a window peeper.

Greg drove down to Ford Parkway and headed west past the Ford Plant. When he glanced at the speedometer, the needle was quivering at sixty. He smashed his fist into the steering wheel a couple of times, so hard that at first he thought he'd broken his hand. Then he put his head down momentarily, and he howled.

He'd heard a sound like that when he tried to pick up his black Labrador from the street after the puppy had been hit by a car, when Greg was nine years old.

The Old Lady's Guest Book

. . . .

*I*T WAS A sunny Saturday afternoon in October, and I was in an ornery mood as I sped down Highway I-94 toward Minneapolis. There would be only a few more warm days like this before the raw winds of November came, and I felt I was wasting this one visiting Aunt Emma. She was a hundred and one years old and had been in a nursing home for the past seven years. I'd known her for more than forty years, ever since I was a kid growing up in eastern Wisconsin. She'd been a wonderful friend over the years. I'd fished with her, eaten Chinese takeout with her, and helped her plant a garden and nurse an ailing husband. But I wasn't looking forward to our visit, another item on my list of seemingly endless obligations.

Emma's health had been failing for months. These days she was pretty well confined to her overstuffed chair. Usually she was asleep when I walked in, with the newspaper on her lap and her heavy spectacles perched on the edge of her nose. "Thomas, oh Thomas," she'd say. "Here's my Tommie." I'd tell her about the weather outside. She'd ask about my father, who was also in a nursing home. And I'd ask her how she was feeling. "I'm taking it as it comes," she'd say wearily. "It's a gay old life if you don't weaken."

Sometimes, after we'd sat silently together, Emma would sit up in her chair and lean toward me, reaching for my hands. She'd grab them and pull me closer to her. "You know," she'd whisper, "I've lived long enough. I'm ready to go. Why can't I go, Tommie?" I never had an answer. She'd been a great lady, all right, full of adventure and spunk and joy, but I felt all of that was gone, and the memories were getting harder and harder to recall.

Emma never seemed to be able to remember anyone's visits. If I was taking the trouble to see her, then I wanted her to know I'd been there. I also wanted the other family members to know that I'd been doing my duty. So on this visit, I brought a small notebook, an "assorted color paper Li'l Big Book" that I'd purchased for ninety-five cents at the corner drugstore. After I kissed Emma and we exchanged pleasantries, I said, "Aunt Emma, here's a little guest book so your visitors can sign in. Now you'll know who's coming to see you." She thanked me several times. I stayed for half an hour, watching the clock radio behind her. As I left, I reminded her to tell her visitors about the guest book so they could record their visits. I wrote the first entry: "10/10. Thomas was here."

When I came back the next week, Emma seemed about the same: tired, weak, and detached. We chatted about my job, my father, and the food at the nursing home. I knew she'd say it was bad and there was too much of it. After five minutes I asked Emma whether

anyone had signed her guest book. It was tucked in the cushion of her chair. I was surprised to find half a dozen pages of written notes by family members and someone named Linda.

"10/12. Linda K. was here. I'm glad Emma is on my floor. I enjoy her, and I love to listen to her stories. I admire her spunk. She is a vivacious lady, and I want to be just like her when I grow up. Ha ha. Lately she has been feeling weak and is using more and more oxygen, but she still enjoys her visits and reading the paper. She got her hair done yesterday, and I told her she looked just great. Boy, did she crack a big smile. Emma, I respect you, and I love you."

"Who's Linda?" I asked.

Emma looked at me vacantly for a moment and then smiled broadly. Linda was a practical nurse. Emma said she had a daughter and that was about all she knew of her. "But she's pretty darned smart," Emma added, "and she's a good listener. I hope I'm not boring her."

A business trip took me out of town for a couple of weeks, and when I visited Emma again, she was slumped in her chair, with her head on her chest. Gently, I shook her shoulder. She was wheezing as she struggled to breathe. She looked into my face. Suddenly she smiled and took my hand.

"Oh, my Tommie's here," she whispered. "I'm so glad you came to see me." I asked her how she'd been. "Oh, I'm still here, but that's about it. I can't seem to remember anything from day to day."

I chuckled and opened her guest book. There were several new entries from Linda.

"10/18. Emma told me she feels she is just a big bother and no one should have to take the time with her. But all she needs is a little tender loving care. That's one of the reasons I became a nurse—to give support and comfort to those who need it. And sooner or later we all do. I started the oxygen at 4L/min. Noted some swelling in her feet and put them on the recliner. Emma seems comfortable and reasonably content. She told me today she wishes the Lord would take her, but He must think she has work to do yet. Well, it's almost noon. Where does the time go? It seems I just got here. Dear Lord, please be with Emma. She is such a dear lady.

"10/20. Emma is in her bed today. She got stuck in the railing when she tried to get out of bed. It just breaks my heart. She's okay, though, and is going to stay in bed for a day or two. She is really something. Bless her.

"10/22. Well, winter is here. My car was covered with a dusting of snow, and it looked so beautiful. It's beautiful to look at but not fun to drive in or scrape. Emma, you look wonderful. You got your hair fixed yesterday, and you seem so peaceful today.

"10/24. Emma wants me to write in here today. She says, 'I'm in a terrible mood. Everything is going to pot.' She is full of piss and vinegar. I love it. She yelled about her dentures being chipped and her glasses not being clean enough and anything else she could think of. I don't blame her. Who else does she have to take her frustrations out on? Dear, dear Emma. I believe she wants to leave this world and go on to the next, but she has work to do yet. Maybe an example of a spunky liberated woman is what the world needs to see. There is a reason God wants her with us, and I'm so happy. Thank you, Lord, for Emma's example of strength, wisdom, contentment, and beauty."

I closed the notebook and looked at Emma, and tears welled in my eyes. Carefully I folded my arms around her tiny body and told her I loved her. I thanked her for all of the good times and asked her to tell me a story from the days when she was young, before I was born.

"Did I ever tell you," she said without hesitation, "about how I learned to use a fly rod? It was up at Bay Lake on a trip with the other seamstresses in the tailor shop where I worked. One young man was standing on the dock casting a small streamer with his fly rod. It was pretty to watch. He'd just wave that rod, and the line would go shooting out, so straight and far. He caught a dozen crappies, big slabs. He saw me watching and asked if I wanted to try. I told him I didn't think I could do it, but he gave me the rod and stood behind me and took my arm. 'Just move it like a buggy whip,' he told me. Fifteen minutes later I was catching crappies."

Emma's eyes were bright, and she was sitting forward in her chair. "What did the young fellow look like?" I asked.

"Tall, with curly brown hair."

"Did you two ever do more than stand on the dock and fish?"

"Oh, go on with you," she said. "That's none of your business."

This time more than an hour had passed when I said I had to leave, but I'd be back next week.

She replied, as she always did, "Come when you can."

On the way out past the nurse's station I asked whether Linda was on duty. The receptionist paged her. Linda was handsome, small, blond, probably in her thirties, with brown eyes and just enough lines to give her face character.

We shook hands, and she said, "You must be Emma's nephew, the one she's always talking about."

"I want to thank you," I said, "for being so wonderful to Aunt Emma. Your love is amazing."

"I'm the one who's grateful," she said. "Your aunt is teaching *me* about life and love. You're lucky to have had all that time with Emma."

"You know," I said, "you've helped me realize that with more certainty than ever before."

Just then she spotted a light outside one of the rooms and with a wave goodbye hurried down the hall. I walked to my car in the crisp, fall night air, feeling at peace with myself.

After that when I visited with Emma, the first thing I did was read Linda's notes, sprinkled among the greetings from other family members. There weren't very many of us, and Linda wrote the most. She reported that Emma was using oxygen almost every day, that her dentures were sent out for repair and it took a week to fix them and that she was becoming more forgetful and couldn't make phone calls by herself anymore.

I noticed the scrawled handwriting of a new writer in Emma's book.

"11/17. I'm visiting Emma, talking about life and the goals I have for myself. She got a kick out of me being 22 years old when my mother is only 38. Emma has been doing fine today, been sleeping a lot, but no oxygen. She has talked about being 101 years old and how she has led a nice life. She asked about her friend Millie on the second floor. I wish the best for Emma. May God look over her while she's here and after she's gone. I love that woman and will miss her when her time comes. I spent about 30 minutes in here, talking and holding hands, telling each other secrets. William H., nurse's aide."

So the old lady had another friend on the staff, a twenty-two-year-old kid. Twenty-two was my age when I came to Minneapolis after college. Emma was one of the reasons I came.

"11/19. Well, it's my last day with Emma. Tomorrow we switch groups. She hasn't felt that good today and has been sleeping most of the day. She asked me if I had any brothers or sisters, and I said no. She says my mom must spoil me. We both got a good laugh off of that. She's having a snack now, enjoying a cookie and a cup of coffee. She can only eat a little piece at a time, so I break off little pieces. She told me she would like to go to bed early. It's 7:20 now, and Emma's going to bed, says she wants to get a good night's rest. I told her I would see her in the morning. She says, 'Tell your mom what a good son you are.' Then I gave her a kiss on the cheek. William H."

I closed the little book and looked at Emma, dozing in her chair.

"Emma," I said softly, "tell me about your new friend William." She opened her eyes. I moved closer. "Tell about William."

"He's such a nice young man," she said, waving a hand in front of her face. "You know, he's colored. He holds my hand. And his mother's only thirty-eight years old."

"He's young enough to be your great-great-grandson."

"Go on with you," she said, "but if I did have a grandson, I couldn't have one better than William."

Right after Christmas I met William. He was tall, with darting brown eyes and a perpetual smile, and muscular enough to lift Emma with one arm. I thanked him for being so kind to her, and he said the pleasure was his. I kept wondering how a kid could have such a generous spirit. When I was his age, old folks were not of my world.

After the first of the year, Emma deteriorated rapidly. Her breathing grew more shallow, she developed a persistent cough, her ankles swelled, and large purple bruises appeared on her arms and legs. Life was a constant misery, and she said she wanted to die. I told her I'd pray for that.

On a Sunday afternoon in January the nursing supervisor phoned to say that Emma was dying. When I got to the home, Emma was on her back in bed with a washcloth on her forehead. Without her false teeth, her face was sunken. Her eyes were closed. I told her I loved her, and I could hear her whisper the words back to me. I pulled a chair next to her bed and opened the guest book almost unconsciously.

"1/22. Dear Emma, I know I have to say goodbye to you, but it's so very hard to realize that I will not see you or hug you and talk with you. I truly love you, and you have added so much joy to my life. I will never, never forget you and what a high-spirited and terrific woman you were—and always will be. God bless you. I'm thankful for the time we had. Linda K."

"1/23. Well, I have been in to check on Emma about every two hours. She's still going. I've talked to her a couple of times and told her I was here, and she'd say, 'William, oh William,' and I'd say, 'I'm here, Emma.' I told her I loved her very much, God bless her. I'm going to miss her when she's gone, but I had a wonderful time while she was here. I'm never going to forget Emma, and I hope she never forgets me. I cried so hard yesterday when I was in here to see her. It hurts so bad. Linda said she cried too. It's 2:10 p.m., and I'm sitting in here, holding her hand. I don't want to let go. But I think she does. William H."

Twelve hours later Emma died peacefully in her sleep.

Bend Over, Please

· ·

*R*AY WAS still half asleep when he raised the toilet lid to take a piss. Five seconds later he was wide awake. The end of his penis felt as if it were on fire, as if it had been dipped in a beaker of sulfuric acid, as if his urine stream were boring a new hole. The pain took his breath away, and his eyes watered. He sat on the toilet, hoping that might make the process a little easier. It didn't. As he shaved and showered, he recalled basic training at Fort Leonard Wood and the guys talking about the clap. But Ray had been married for fifteen years and, as the vows said, had kept only unto his wife. This wasn't the clap, he decided.

His wife had left early to take the kids to school, so Ray skipped breakfast and hurried to work. The first thing he did was call his doctor.

"Dr. McCallum's not in today and won't be back until next week," the receptionist said.

"I need to see a doctor right away."

"Okay, Dr. Langer is in and has a cancellation at two-thirty. Be sure to be here on time."

"That won't be a problem."

Ray was at the clinic at two-fifteen. By then he had urinated again, and the second time was as painful as the first. The waiting room was full. Ray sat in a straight-back wooden chair with rounded slats that dug into the small of his back. Across the room a mother was trying to control her screaming child. When Ray looked at her, she pointed to her ear, apparently to indicate the kid had an ear infection. For a moment Ray thought about pointing to the site of his discomfort; instead, he offered a weak smile.

He was still in his chair at three o'clock, trying to develop interest in a *Sports Afield* cover story, "Topwater Bass—The Predators of the Shallows." He was thinking about a trip to the men's room to take another leak when he heard his name. The nurse ushered him into a tiny examining room. He sat on the chair next to the desk and flipped through a pamphlet on hypertension. There was a tap on the door, and a young woman in a white coat walked in. She was beautiful, with brown hair loose around her shoulders, hazel eyes, full lips, and a tan face that highlighted the whiteness of her teeth.

"I'm Diane Langer," she said. "How can I help you?"

"Well, I've been in pretty good health, you know, generally. I'm trying to eat right and get exercise and, you know, do the stuff you're supposed to do when you hit forty." He was babbling as though he were in high school and had run into one of the cheerleaders in the hall. "I've got a little high blood pressure, and I like to have it checked regularly. So I thought I'd do that now, you know?"

She slipped the inflatable cuff on his arm and squeezed the bulb. "Looks good," she said. "One hundred and thirty over eighty. That's not bad." She sat on a tall stool in front of him. "The nurse said you had to see a doctor today," she said. "It must be something besides your blood pressure."

He felt a flush creep over his face. "You're right," he said, "it's not my blood pressure. It's something in my urinary tract. When I pee, it burns like hell. I don't think it's a venereal disease or anything, since I haven't been sexually active. No, I mean I'm sexually active, you know, but with my wife."

"It's probably a prostate infection," Dr. Langer said. "Let's get a urine sample."

She left the room, and a nurse brought him a plastic container. Ray forced himself to urinate briefly. He opened the door, and the nurse collected the sample. In a few minutes Dr. Langer returned.

"You've got an infection, all right," she said. "There are a few pus cells in the sample." Ray cringed. It was such an unsavory condition: pus in the urine. He reminded himself the woman in front of him with a stethoscope around her neck wasn't his prom date. She was a damned doctor. "I need to check that prostate gland," she continued.

She turned away while Ray dropped his shorts. Asking him to stand in front of the examining table, she uttered the dread command: "Would you bend over, please." Her initial thrust caused him to gulp, but she was quick and much gentler than his usual doctor.

43

"The gland is swollen," she reported, snapping off her latex glove. "I'm going to give you a prescription for a sulfa drug. And I'd like you to lay off alcohol for a couple of weeks. Also, it'd be a good idea to avoid sexual activity for a week." Ray blushed again. He tucked his shirt in his pants while Dr. Langer wrote out a prescription. She handed him the slip and smiled.

"It's good to meet you," she said. "You should get relief in a day or so."

Ray reached for her hand and shook it. "I'm glad to meet you, and thanks for being so, you know, under-standing and all."

That evening he sat at the kitchen table fiddling with his bottle of pills until his wife asked about the prescrip-tion. He told her the whole story, not omitting a single detail.

She paused from shredding lettuce to congratulate him on being a nineties kind of guy. "But if you're looking for a medal," she said, "stand in line. There are millions of women, including me, ahead of you."

"But the point is," he said, "she is a beautiful woman. That brings the sexual tension element into the picture."

"So it's good looks that makes the difference? Well, you don't know what my gynecologist looks like. Did you ever wonder?"

Ray didn't answer. He opened his prescription bottle, shook out a couple of yellow capsules, and popped them in his mouth. He walked to the sink, got a glass of water and swallowed.

Let's Just Talk

. . . .

*I*T WAS A LUXURY to take a shower in the old, yellow, wooden barracks at Fort Leonard Wood—all by yourself. I felt good as I let the hot water run over my head and shoulders. The workday was over, and basic training was behind me. I was now a part of a vehicle-maintenance battery, a group of young citizen-soldiers who were going to learn to change the oil and tune the engines of jeeps and transport trucks.

How in the hell I landed in such an outfit mystified me since I barely knew how to open the hood of my '51 Pontiac. But that was in another world, a world of high school, basketball games, and weekend beer parties. This was the army, where even eighteen-year-olds like me were expected to act like men who knew what they were doing. I thought I'd done pretty well at behaving like a man, especially since I looked fifteen. I'd made some friends here in Charlie Company, guys who were five or six years older, had real jobs, and had gone to college, like I was intending to do.

One of my buddies was George, a mechanic who had worked in his father's garage in Clear Lake, Iowa, before he got drafted. George was big, maybe six feet four, two hundred and thirty pounds, and now I noticed his bulk standing next to me, twisting his head under the shower spigot to get some water on his face.

"Say," he said with a big grin, "a bunch of us are going to town tonight, to the Kit Kat Club. How about coming along?"

"Nah, it's been a long week, it's raining like hell, and I don't feel like getting drunk."

George laughed, a dull roar rumbling from his gut. "We ain't going to the Kitty Club to get drunk, boy. We're going to get laid. I mean, you do want to be with a woman, don't you?"

How was I going to tell him I was a virgin? Oh yeah, I made out in the back seat with Jane a lot last year, even French-kissed her and got her bra off once. I thought about it a lot, and I wanted to do it, but the thought of having sex with a stranger, for money, was scary.

George got the idea. "Look," he said, "if you're a cherry, don't worry about it. These ladies are real special, and we'll find one who'll teach you the ropes. Come on, you owe it to yourself. Shit, you're a soldier now."

"No, I ain't a virgin," I lied. "It's just that I've never been to a whorehouse before."

George said there was a first time for everything and told me to be ready by seven-thirty. Dave was going, and so was Pete.

I said I'd be ready. I went back to my bunk, sat on my footlocker, and tried to figure out what I'd gotten myself into. I put on a pair of chinos, a short-sleeved shirt, and my cowboy boots with the high heels. I knew I looked young, but I didn't want to look so short. I combed my hair and splashed on some aftershave. Maybe this wouldn't be so bad. I was a long way from home, and nobody but me would know, and maybe this was a real nice place where they served cold beer and had a nice little band and I could find a young one who looked like Sandra Dee. I'd seen *A Summer Place* a couple of times, and thinking about her, with those full lips, always gave me an erection. Maybe she'd be real gentle, she'd take off my clothes as we sat on the bed, and she'd put on some music—a Johnny Mathis album. And maybe when we got through, she'd tell me I'd been one of the best men she'd ever been with.

George poked his head in the door. "We're ready. Let's go."

It was raining on the way into Waynesville. George's car was filled with the nervous braggadocio of young men. "You just wait, little buddy," Dave told me. "There's nothing like getting your pipes cleaned. You'll have something to tell the college crowd about."

"We're fixing you up with Waynesville Mary," Pete said. "She's so tough and so homely that afterward you get a pin that says, 'I Made It with Mary.'"

From the outside the Kit Kat Club looked like one of those corner taverns in the Wisconsin countryside where I grew up. It was a small white clapboard building with a red neon Budweiser sign flashing in the window. Inside at the bar were a half-dozen guys, mostly soldiers, judging from their haircuts. Across the room was an empty pool table. Patsy Cline's "Crazy" was blaring from the jukebox. The cigarette smoke was so thick my eyes started to water. I couldn't see a woman in the place. The four of us sat on folding chairs at a table in one corner. George went up to the bar and came back with four beers.

"I don't see any women," I said.

"No," George said. "They work out of a couple trailers in the back." George had talked to the bartender about the girls. We had to pay thirty-five dollars each, in advance. I gave him the money. He said, "Save another five bucks for a tip. It's a good idea, in case you ever want to come back."

We headed out the bar's back door. It was still raining. George led the way to one of the trailers. He said he and Pete would go in first, since two of the four girls were already with "clients." That left Dave and me standing out in the rain, the kind of cold rain that comes in the fall. My shoes, my highly shined army-issue black oxfords, were spattered with mud. Suddenly I wanted to go, to bolt, but it was too late.

"Maybe," Dave said, "we'll get the best looking ones—you know, saving the best for the best." After about five minutes the trailer door opened. A woman in the doorway flicked a cigarette onto the wet ground. "Next," she said.

"You go," Dave said. "I'll wait for the next one." I trudged up the steps into the trailer. She was wearing a tank top and Bermuda shorts. She was in her late thirties, I guessed. She wasn't pretty. Her face was too wide, her lips were too thin and her teeth were too crooked. She sure didn't look like Sandra Dee. Her smile seemed gentle and understanding, though.

She led me toward one of the trailer's bedrooms. The place was dark. It smelled like a fish-cleaning shack. She motioned for me to sit on the bed, and she closed the door.

"They call me Kate," she said softly, as she sat on the bed next to me. "Now you tell me what I can do for you."

"Well, I don't want you to take this personally, but I don't think I want to do anything but talk. I'm just kind of not in the mood tonight. And I don't want my friends to know that we didn't do anything, you know?"

She said she understood and told me to take my shoes off and lie down on the bed. "Don't worry, all we'll do is talk." She lay next to me and put her arm on my chest. "Now, why don't you tell me about yourself."

I told her I had just graduated from high school and had joined the army for six months of active duty before going to college. I said I maybe was going to be a journalist or a writer. "In high school I always liked to write, and I was good in English. I also liked music, but I wasn't very good at it. I play the trombone, but I'm better at the scales than on the songs. I guess you'd say I'm a technician."

She rolled over, shook a cigarette from the pack on the nightstand, and lit it with a kitchen match. She lay back again, stared at the ceiling, and let the smoke drift from her nostrils. "I got a daughter who plays the clarinet," she said. "And she's good. She's in the concert band."

"How old is she?"

"Twelve."

"What's her name?

"Jennifer."

She took a drag on her cigarette. "Yeah, Jennifer is a real good kid, kind of like you. I imagine you were always a good boy."

"Well, I used to raise a little hell," I said. "We'd get drunk now and then, and I wrecked my dad's car once."

She rolled over and looked right at me. "If you're going to be a writer, what are you going to write about?"

I said I didn't know, but maybe I'd write about people who did what most people didn't do.

"That sounds like me," she said. "What would you write about me?"

"Well, I'd say you're a nice person, that you got a daughter you love."

"What would you say about what I do?"

"I guess I'd say you're a prostitute, but I don't know why."

"No, you don't, do you?"

Then she told me she'd been married. Her husband had been in the army and he would come home drunk.

He would beat her with a razor strap and threaten to hurt Jennifer. She had him arrested, and the army booted him out. Now he was in a veteran's hospital with cirrhosis. "I didn't have any money after he was gone," she said, "and I didn't have very many skills, either. We got married while I was still in high school. I guess what I'm saying is I did what I had to do. And, I've never taken one dime of welfare, not one dime."

We could hear a lot of moaning and thrashing around in the next bedroom. She said, "You haven't changed your mind, sweetie, have you?"

"No," I said, "I got my money's worth."

I started to get up. She stopped me and took my hands in hers. "You know, you're a real nice young guy. You save it for some nice young gal. And don't worry, you're a man. You're more of a man than most of them who come here."

I put my shoes on and reached for my wallet. I took out five dollars. "Here, I want you to have this, for being so nice and all."

"Keep your money," she said. The look on her face was almost shy, and gentle. "Your buddies will probably ask you what I did for you. You tell them this." She put her arms around me and whispered in my ear. Jesus, I got weak in the knees. She laughed and shook out a cigarette from her pack of Pall Mall's on the nightstand and gave it to me along with a book of matches. "Take this. Most guys like one now."

George and Pete were waiting outside. She kissed me on the cheek as we stood on the tiny stoop. "You take care," she said.

When I walked down the steps, George put his arm around my shoulder. "I'm proud of you, boy. How was it?"

"I don't know," I said. "It was like nothing I ever felt before." I put the cigarette in my lips, fired up, and inhaled. I almost choked to death.

The Beaver Pond

. . . .

*T*HERE WERE two of them, boys twelve or thirteen
years old, standing on a couple of big pine logs at
the edge of the beaver pond. They had spinning rods
and were flipping tiny lures out into the dark, tamarack-colored water. Suddenly one of them let out a
whoop and ran down the shore.

"I got another one," he hollered, as a brown trout
jumped a foot out of the water.

From where I was standing about a hundred yards
away, it appeared to be a two-pounder. I walked down
from the stand of birch and reached them as they were
putting the fish on a stringer, along with two others of
exactly the same size. I said hello, and the boys turned
around, startled.

"Do you guys know you're fishing on private
property?"

"Well, mister," the smaller boy said, "we didn't
know who owned it. And this is only the second time
we've been here." He had a blond crew cut and an in-
fectious smile. The other boy, with the brim of his old
brown felt hat pulled stylishly over his eyes, said, "We
discovered the pond by accident when we were looking for my dog that ran off in the woods. The thing is,
we saw these trout breaking water and feeding all over

the pond. We just had to come back. Are you the owner?"

"No, but I'm a friend of his. I'm up here for the day to plant some tulip bulbs for him and his wife."

"Does he fish here?" the smaller boy asked.

"No, and it's not likely he'll ever get the chance."

"Why?"

So I told them about Bryan and his beaver pond.

About a year ago I visited Bryan in a Saint Paul hospital. He's a doctor who served with a Special Forces team in Vietnam. He's written dozens of articles for medical journals and lectured all over the world on how to treat premature babies. But he's an ordinary guy, who likes just about everybody he meets. And he likes bulldogs, fast cars, tractors, and boxing matches. That day in the hospital Bryan was a patient, recovering from surgery to remove a cancerous tumor in his colon. But the cancer had spread, and he was to begin chemotherapy in a week. He was sitting up in bed when I walked in, and he greeted me with a nonchalant hello.

"I'm sorry the news is bad," I said. "I know you're a scrapper, and I want to be along on your ride."

"Yeah," he said, "it's kind of a kick in the ass. But we're all heading there, you know? I'm just going to get there quicker."

He told me about his idea for planting some trout or bass in the beaver pond on his property in the jackpine country of western Wisconsin, but he didn't know how to go about it. I said I'd call the Department of Natural Resources for the names of some local fish hatcheries. A week later I brought him a list of a dozen hatcheries, along with enough information on bass and trout to start his own fish management program.

That summer Bryan gained strength during a remission from the cancer in his gut. He continued his medical research and writing. He looked for an Indy race car to buy. He cut new walking trails at his cabin. And he attended the obligatory social occasions, full of his usual charm and good humor. But he didn't get around to stocking the pond, and he didn't mention it again, until almost a year later, when he was back in the hospital again. This time they cut out more of his gut and put a bag on his side. Bryan was a big man who had always taken care of his body: he biked, he ran, he swam. He'd kept that body intact during the last year, but he couldn't do it much longer.

"So, how are you doing?" I asked, as I walked into his hospital room, where he was hooked up to complex monitors whose red, blinking numbers told secrets I couldn't fathom.

Bryan looked at me for a moment, as though waiting for his eyes to focus. "Let's put it this way," he said quietly. "It ain't the ninth inning yet, but I'm in the bottom of the seventh."

"If there's anything I can do, let me know."

"There's one thing," he said. "I'm planning to stock

some brown trout in the beaver pond. And I'd like to have you there when we do it. Sometime next month, on a Saturday."

On the last Saturday in April, a warm sunny day, my wife and I headed north on Highway 35. There were half a dozen shades of new green on the bushes, shrubs, and birch trees on the sand hills and river valleys of the rolling countryside, after a long and bitterly cold winter. I rolled down the car window to let in the crisp, clean air.

When we arrived at the cabin, Bryan's wife, Jean, greeted us and led us to the back porch, where Bryan was sitting in a canvas chair with his feet propped up on the railing. He looked grayer, thinner, and weaker. His eyes had a vacant look, as though part of him had taken leave. Nevertheless, he asked us about our jobs and the garden and Gabriel, our fat white cat.

The phone rang, and Jean announced that the man from the fish hatchery would meet us on the fire trail near the pond. The four of us piled into Bryan's four-wheeler, and we got there before the hatchery tank truck. My wife and Jean took a walk. Bryan and I sat on a log, and for five minutes, without saying anything, we stared at the pond, the towering white pine on the far end, the little island in the middle, and the broad light-green leaves of the emerging water lilies in the shallows.

"I've always liked the way this place looks," Bryan said at last. "It has a kind of symmetry to it. It's been here at least fifty years."

"And it'll probably be here a lot longer than we will," I said and immediately regretted the remark.

"You know," he said, "this life of mine has been a goddamn adventure. If anything seemed worth trying, I tried it."

"That's what I've always liked about you," I said.

"I have an old friend who sold a business and then started another of the same kind. Hell, he did that once, and he did it well. Why not try something new?"

I shrugged. Neither of us looked at each other. We sat side by side, but we talked to the pond. Somehow, it seemed easier that way.

"You know," Bryan said, "we're going to have to carry these trout from the truck to the pond in buckets. And I don't have the strength to do it."

"That's why we're here. You take the pictures, and we'll carry the fish."

We heard the rumble of a diesel engine through the woods, and soon the hatchery truck pulled up at the end of the fire trail. The hatchery man was a

Finlander, a smiling fellow with an ample belly. As Bryan walked off to find our wives, I hopped up to the tank in the bed of the truck and lifted the cover. I had been expecting to see fingerlings, slightly bigger than walleye minnows for fishing, but these trout were two-pounders, maybe more, huge German browns with dark green on their sides and crimson splotches above their bellies. They were beautiful, full of energy and strength.

"How come such big fish?" I asked the hatchery man.

"Well, your friend there told me he didn't have too much time to watch these grow. He wanted the biggest trout I had. I even threw in some of my brood stock. These browns are good for a beaver pond. They tend to stay at home, even in high water. So these fish are going to be around for a while."

Jean and my wife and I began the bucket haul. Bryan sat on a log on a hillside with his camera. He was exhausted after clambering up on the truck to see the fish. As the women carried the first pails of fish the fifty yards to the pond, I stood next to the truck and watched, struck by the brilliant blue of the day and the sadness of my mood, as though I were looking at a delicate water color of two women carrying fish to a pond, watched by a dreamer whose thoughts I couldn't begin to imagine.

"Hey," the hatchery man said, "are you going to carry a pail or what?"

I grabbed a pail of trout and walked slowly down

the path to the pond, thinking of biblical references to fish—Peter the fisherman, the fish at the Sermon on the Mount—and the eternal nature of things—birth, death, new life. When I got to the edge of the pond, I heaved the trout into the air. The trout arched in the sunlight gleaming off their backs. When they hit the water, they darted ahead. Before I turned toward the truck, some of them were jumping. They were home, soon to be searching for minnows. Maybe some of them would spawn there, producing a generation of native fish.

It took us about an hour to stock the four hundred pounds of trout, pail by pail. Our arms were weary. When the tank was empty, Bryan walked over to the Finlander. "Well," he said, "I think it's time to settle up. How much do I owe you?" I didn't stick around for the answer because it was none of my business and Bryan had never made a show of spending money. He wrote out a check on the hood of the truck and handed it to the hatchery man.

"Try it in the morning and the evening," the man said. "That's when these babies like to feed on minnows. They're a little more persnickety than rainbows, but you can catch them. Small copper spoons work the best."

The two young trespassers sitting next to me knew that. Each of them had a copper spoon or spinner on his rod. As they stood up to leave, the taller boy asked if I wanted them to let the trout go.

"No, keep them," I said, "but if you fish here again don't keep more than a couple, and let the bigger ones go. And don't tell anyone about the beaver pond."

They nodded, picked up the stringer and their poles, and walked off to where the creek came tumbling out of the pond. I lost sight of them as they scrambled through a stand of alders alongside the creek.

They walked out of the woods with more than the trout. They had another secret and a couple of promises to keep. Somehow, I believed they would. Hell, I knew they would. I turned back to the beaver pond, which by now looked like sparkling ginger ale in the late-afternoon sun.

No One Gets to Lead

. . . .

*I*T WASN'T starting out as the romantic second honeymoon Kent had hoped it would be. He and Jennifer were weaving through the crowd and searching for the baggage claim at San Francisco International Airport. Kent was sweaty and tired and in dire need of taking a piss. He spotted a men's room sign.

"Hang onto my bag," he said. "Too much coffee."

He was momentarily struck by how tired Jenny was looking. She was still pretty, though, with her brown eyes, chiseled features, and ready smile, the sign that they were, as she put it, connecting.

They hadn't done much connecting lately, Kent thought, as he stared blankly at the graffiti-covered wall behind the urinal. In fact, after ten years of marriage they were like strangers who couldn't make it past the small talk about the weather. He had to admit that these days he was relieved at bedtime when Jennifer turned out the lights and went to sleep. He still wanted her physically, but there was a distance, an angry, persistent gap between them.

Someone tapped him on the shoulder. He jerked his head around. A stocky man wearing a cowboy hat said, "I'm sorry to bother you, pardner, but I got to take a leak in the worst way."

Kent zipped up his fly, washed his hands, and hurried out the door. He took Jenny's hand as they headed downstairs to the baggage carousels. Jennifer had refused to carry her bag on the plane, claiming that there was never enough room in the overhead bins. So here they were waiting, Jennifer watching for her bag on the luggage merry-go-round. Kent leaned against a pillar, arms folded, staring at the other waiting travelers. If she'd listened to him, by now they'd be in a cab on their way to the Holiday Inn. Kent caught himself clenching his jaw and grinding his teeth. Jesus, he wondered, what the hell was he worrying about? They'd been waiting only a few minutes, and there were a dozen empty cabs lined up outside—it wasn't as if they'd missed the last ride downtown. Kent made up his mind not to get bitchy over the delay and eased beside Jennifer at the carousel, slipping his arm around her waist.

"They must have put my bag on first," she said, "and naturally it's going to be the last one off."

He shrugged and, without thinking, shot back, "Well, if you'd listened to me and carried the bag, it wouldn't have happened."

Jennifer's body stiffened. When she spied her maroon bag, she grabbed it, slung it over her shoulder, and hurried toward the cabs.

Their driver's bald head was covered by a Greek fisherman's cap, and his barrel chest was draped with a T-shirt that read, "San Francisco—The World's Most Romantic City." As he lurched out into the traffic flow, the cabbie turned around and looked at Jennifer. "First time in San Francisco?" he asked. When she smiled and shook her head, he said, "Well, if you haven't seen it for awhile, it's still as beautiful. There are more beggars on the streets. But it's still, you know, a city for lovers."

Kent didn't feel much like a lover. He felt more like a loner who maybe didn't belong married. He'd been single for almost ten years after his divorce, and he'd become used to his own rhythms and routines. He had just about convinced himself that he was programmed to live alone, like a guy in a Frank Sinatra song up at dawn on a gray Sunday morning waiting for the paperboy. But then he met Jennifer at a dinner party. She was the nursing director at a Twin Cities hospital. She was bright and sensual and outspoken and honest. She told the truth without being hurtful or accusatory. As the months went by in their courtship, he decided she loved him flaws and all. And he loved her.

Why then was he now feeling so estranged, so at odds with her all the time? It was as though he was always fighting for control to preserve his manhood. Yet Jen always supported him and never begrudged him time with his friends. The problem was for him to yield the autonomy she demanded. He was a child of the fifties, when husbands came home to dinner on the table and wives organized the Junior League charity auction. And lately the gender-role rigmarole seemed to be insinuating itself in his reactions to everything and everybody, as in a recent confrontation with his father when he went back home to see him. Jennifer had sent his father a birthday card and pasted one of her return-address stickers on the envelope. It had her maiden name, which she had kept in their marriage.

"Why didn't she take the family name?" his father asked him.

"She'd already made a name for herself at the hospital and among her friends, and she didn't want to give it up. And that's perfectly all right with me."

"Well, it's not all right with me," his father said. "It's like our name isn't good enough for her."

"The world's changing, Pa. Women need their own identity and the name is part of it. She couldn't love me more, or better, if she took my name."

"It's a slap in the face to our family. I can't understand why you can't see that."

Jennifer was shaking his arm. "Kent, the cab driver's asking if we like seafood and want some recommendations for dinner." He was momentarily embarrassed, vaguely recalling that the cabbie had been chattering away since they left the airport.

"You bet," Kent said. "The last seafood we had was at Scoma's on the Wharf, and we about had to take out a second mortgage to pay the bill."

"You go to Tadich's," the driver said. "It's not fancy, and you and the missus may have to wait for a table, but the sole and salmon are great—less than twelve bucks each."

By the time they reached the Holiday Inn at the edge of Chinatown, Kent and Jennifer were talking civilly. As they unpacked in their room overlooking the Bay and Alcatraz, Kent took Jennifer's hands and led her over to the window.

"I'm sorry for being so short-tempered," he said. "I really want to make the best of this trip."

"I'll try, too," she said.

For several days they walked, climbed, and ate their way across the city from North Beach to Nob Hill to Fisherman's Wharf. At Pier 39 on the wharf they watched the sea lions struggling to pull their blubbery bulk up on the floating dock to doze in the sun. One of the older bulls barked and nipped at a younger rival hoisting himself onto the pier. At the last moment the old bull nudged with his nose to send him sprawling and splashing back in the water.

"It reminds me of the chief of pediatrics," Jennifer said, "when he makes rounds with one of his young residents."

At the House of Nanking, a hole-in-the-wall Chinese restaurant a block from their hotel, where they waited in line with men in business suits carrying briefcases and kids in jeans wearing backpacks, the extensive menu was a sham. The customers' only choices were chicken, pork, or seafood, hot and spicy or just spicy. Jennifer liked to ask how the dish was prepared, with what ingredients, and if she could get the sauce on the side. She reminded Kent of the Meg Ryan character in the movie *When Harry Met Sally*, another high-maintenance woman. They were seated at the counter, and Jennifer asked the harried waitress about the cashew chicken.

"Is it spicy? What kind of oil is it cooked in?"

"So, missy," the waitress replied, "you trust Nanking. We make spicy chicken dish. You like. You eat. You happy."

Afterward Jennifer pronounced the chicken excellent and insisted that they leave a big tip. Kent was pleased with Jennifer's generosity and adventurous spirit.

That was the reason, he decided, they were now heading north across the Golden Gate Bridge in a rented Pontiac, bound for a bed and breakfast in redwood country. Jennifer heard about the Benbow Inn from a bellhop, who told her it was charming and peaceful, and had the best cinnamon-raisin-apple oatmeal in the world. Kent's first thought was that two hundred miles was too far to drive to look at some redwood trees and eat a bowl of oatmeal, but he kept his mouth shut. He apparently didn't hide his resentment, though, since Jennifer pointed out he'd hardly said a word all day.

"I'm just trying to get through this traffic without smashing up Mr. Hertz' car."

He flipped on the radio, and they listened in silence to "the best of country" until they rolled into Ukiah, in the heart of Mendocino County's vineyards. Jennifer announced she had to make a pit stop, so Kent pulled into a Shell station at the edge of town. While he was topping off the tank, he looked up at the surrounding hillsides. The dark-green grape vines dotted the hills in neat parallel rows, in a sharp contrast to the brown grass that covered the valley floor. There were gnarled oaks and dry creek beds and dusty roads, reminding him of the scenery in the old Western movies he'd watched as a kid. As they pulled out of town, he told Jennifer that the country struck a nostalgic chord from Saturday afternoon harmonies when he played Roy Rogers to the next-door neighbor boy's Hopalong Cassidy. It had been a long time since anything had made him feel like a kid again—too many responsibilities, too many obligations got in the way.

The only obligation he had this afternoon was to keep the car between the yellow line and the shoulder, which became more tedious as they snaked around the curves of Highway 101 into the King Mountain Range. The rolling vineyards and the dry-grass meadows were replaced with forests and rocky river gorges. Even on this sunny afternoon, fog blanketed some of the hills. In the valleys were groves of redwoods, each with a name: Smithe, Reynolds, Richardson.

"I trust," Kent said, "these were all guys who loved redwood trees."

"Or maybe," Jennifer added, "one was a woman who threw her body in front of a logger's truck."

Kent stopped at the first turnout. The ancient redwoods stretched over two hundred feet into the sky. Their bark was the color of iron ore. The ground was fragrant, cool, and damp, covered with ferns. Sunlight streamed through the forest canopy in lacy shafts of white. At one of the larger trees, Jennifer ran around to the other side and said, "Let's see if we can hold hands. Put your arms around the tree."

He stretched his arms out and hugged the trunk. The bark felt cool and soft against his face. "So put your arms out," he said. He caught her wrist and pulled her close. He hugged her and gently kissed her. Hand in hand, they walked around the tree and decided they'd need at least two more arms to encircle it.

Dusk was settling in as they drove the final few miles to the Benbow Inn. In the distance it looked like an

English country mansion, with its white stucco sides, red brick chimney, and brown shutters. Their room had oak woodwork, an antique chest of drawers, and a small decanter of sherry and crystal wine glasses. To their delight, the room had no telephone or television. After they had showered, they sat by the window, sipping sherry and gazing at the silvery Eel River.

"I read about the Eel in outdoor magazines when I was a kid," he said. "It was the most famous salmon river in the west."

"That's nice," she murmured, putting her arms around his neck. "But what I need more than the history lesson is for you to make love to me."

That night their lovemaking had an urgency and passion reminiscent of their first months together, but it was also slow and sweet and tender.

When they awoke the next morning, they were almost shy with each other. He held her hand as they walked into the dining room for breakfast and sat at a table next to the window.

"I'll have the oatmeal," Jennifer told the waitress. "It does come with raisins and apples? And I'd like skim milk and a little brown sugar on the side."

When the oatmeal arrived, Jennifer raved about the flavor and texture. Kent inhaled his and asked for another. "Eating this stuff," he said, "reminds me of canoeing in the Boundary Waters. You eat like crazy and paddle your ass off."

"As you may recall," she said, "you got plenty of exercise last night."

Over a second cup of coffee they decided to spend the day at Shelter Cove, an isolated beach about twenty-five miles from the inn. They drove up and down and across the small coastal mountains, stopping for a view of the ocean. It was bright turquoise. The green foothills seemed to fall away to the ocean's shore. A ribbon of black sand separated land from water. Large, jagged brown rocks thrust themselves out of the sand.

"There's no one on the beach," Kent said. "We've got the place to ourselves."

They drove down to a gravel lot, a portable toilet, and a sign warning of the undertow. The sand felt cool and firm under their bare feet. The salty breeze was brisk. The morning fog was still clinging to the hill-tops. Brown pelicans skimmed above the water off the beach. And once in a while a curious seal poked its head up, stared intently at them, and then dove and disappeared.

"Honey," Jennifer called, "look at this."

She had found a small brownish-red starfish stranded on the sand. It was still alive, its rays moving slightly. "It's so delicate and beautiful," Jennifer exclaimed, "but the poor thing is going to die."

"That's the way life is," Kent said.

Jennifer wasn't listening. She cradled the starfish in her hands, walked knee-deep into the surf, and let it float free.

They sat side-by-side on the beach. "I want you to know something," he said. "I love you." She nodded, and he gently cupped her face in his hands, his thumbs on her lips. "No," he said, "I mean I love you, not someone I think you ought to be, but the woman you are."

For the first time in their marriage she saw tears stream down his face.

You Hold Her, Dad

. . . .

*T*HE PLANE from Houston to Bogotá was only about a third full, and Dan had three seats to himself. He had a slight headache, and the only thing he knew about Colombia was what he read in the *Star Tribune* about car bombings and drug trafficking, the police who carried machine guns and the bandits who kidnapped the children of wealthy families. But he was about to meet his daughter, Julie, and her new baby, Lisa. For a month Julie had been in Bogotá to adopt an infant girl from a Colombian orphanage. The paperwork and red tape seemed endless as Colombian authorities checked out the prospective parents and how they handled their infants.

Julie's husband had spent the first three weeks with her but then had been called back to the Twin Cities for a business emergency. Julie had phoned late that night from her room in what she described as a cheap but clean downtown hotel.

"Dad," she'd said, "I'd like you to come down here. I can handle everything but the feeling of being so alone."

Dan hadn't felt up to the trip. Since his wife, Susan, died several years ago, he'd done little traveling, and he'd suffered a mild heart attack last year and now took four pills a day to control his blood pressure and cholesterol.

"I'll get down there as soon as I can," he'd said. "Just give me a couple of days to make the arrangements. My passport's still valid, but I'll have to get somebody to watch the house and maybe a kid to cut the lawn."

As he stared out the plane window, Dan knew why he was undertaking this adventure. Julie needed him and he'd felt the need to be closer to his kids and their families, especially since Susan died. He loved his grandchildren but he never seemed quite comfortable with them. He babysat when the kids called and he'd even taken the oldest boys to Valley Fair. But it always seemed more of a duty than fun and it bothered him.

His thoughts were interrupted, momentarily, when the airline steward asked him if he wanted another split of red wine. He said no. Instead he took two Tylenol tablets, as Julie suggested, since Bogotá is eighty-three hundred feet above sea level, and the altitude difference from the Twin Cities can produce a skull-splitting headache. Dan washed down the tablets with a last swig of wine, after raising the glass to the airplane window. "Here's to you, little Lisa. Let's hope your Grandpa knows what he's doing."

At the Bogotá airport, uniformed guards with machine guns herded the passengers into an inspection line for customs. Dan spotted Julie, with her blond hair in a pixie cut, her sparkling blue eyes, her white teeth that had cost him two thousand dollars to have straightened. She was standing behind a barrier, waving and pointing to the man next to her. He was holding the baby, but Dan could hardly see her past the stone-faced customs agent. Slowly one agent after another sorted through his shirts, T-shirts, socks, and shorts. When he was through the customs line, Julie threw her arms around him.

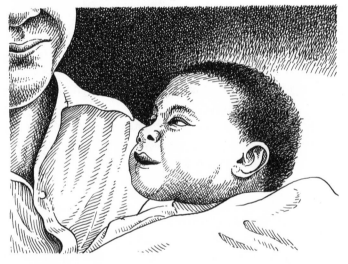

"Honey, are you getting enough to eat?" he asked. "You feel a little thin."

"We're halfway around the earth, Dad, and you're wondering whether I'm eating enough. I'm eating more than usual. This is my driver, Luis, and here's Lisa." Luis handed her the blanketed bundle. "Here, you hold her, Dad."

Gingerly Dan took the child. She had huge brown eyes, a shock of jet-black hair on her forehead, and the tiniest nose and ears. At four months, she was smaller than he'd expected. She was smiling and Dan was surprised at how close he felt to this child he'd never seen.

On the way to the hotel Dan learned why Julie had hired a driver. This traffic made the rush hour at home look like a Sunday afternoon in downtown Saint Paul. There were three lanes of traffic on either side of the car. Luis was shifting lanes, leaning on the horn every minute or so, and shaking his fist at the other drivers. It took him half an hour to reach Julie's hotel, a plain, five-story, stucco building, with no doorman, no bell-hop, no room service.

But her room was big and had two beds and a crib. After dinner and three games of cribbage with Julie, Dan fell into bed and slept soundly. When he awakened at seven the next morning, he could hear Lisa in her crib, making soft, gurgling noises. Julie was eating a bowl of cereal at a table by the window. He could see a box of Cocoa Puffs next to her bowl, the very same stuff she used to eat at home when she was a kid in braces. He kept his eyes half closed, so Julie wouldn't notice he was awake. He wanted to savor the scene and the delicate, early-morning light that flooded the room.

Julie had the day planned. While one of the hotel maids watched the baby, they would visit the orphanage and then arrange for a visa and passport for Lisa. The orphanage was clean, and the staff was friendly. But they had to walk nine flights up to the visa office, wait two hours for Lisa's birth certificate, and deal with five different passport officials. Sitting on a folding chair against the wall in the bare passport office while Julie conferred with a uniformed bureaucrat behind a paper-littered desk, Dan wondered why the kids couldn't have waited a little longer and tried a Minnesota agency.

The next several days were filled with more paperwork, more forms to fill out. Julie tirelessly shuffled from office to office and answered the endless questions. On one of their afternoon walks, as they approached a shopping center near the hotel, Dan noticed half a dozen barefoot children camped in tiny tents on a small patch of grass strewn with cans and papers. The children were five or six years old and were dressed in torn pants and T-shirts. Julie had told him there were upwards of 10,000 street children in Bogotá. One boy with a mud-streaked face was starting a charcoal fire in a tin pail. A naked boy with arms no thicker than broom handles was taking a bath in a public fountain. He soaped his hair, scrubbed his feet and ankles, and dried off with the shirt he'd been wearing. He put on a pair of adult-size jeans, rolling up the cuffs and pulling an old brown belt through the waist loops. There was almost a foot of belt hanging from the buckle.

"At least Lisa won't have to live like this," Dan said. "She'll get a real chance in Minnesota."

"This is Lisa's birth country, Dad, part of her heritage, but you make it sound like some kind of third-world jungle." Dan could tell Julie was angry.

"There are beautiful people here and thousands of years of culture and history. And there are plenty of homeless or runaway children roaming the streets of Minneapolis. I'm not trying to lecture you, Dad, and I'm so glad you're here. I just want you to understand that we're proud of who our baby is and where she comes from."

"I'm sorry, honey."

At three in the afternoon a week after Dan arrived in Bogotá, Julie learned by phone that the adoption was finally approved and all the papers were signed. They could take Lisa home. Dan whirled Julie around the room, and they cried together. He hadn't felt this good even when the doctors told him there was no permanent damage to his heart. Their celebration ended when Lisa started to cry, upset over all the whooping and hollering. That night at the hotel they had a dinner of red wine and pizza, which Dan had persuaded the chef to cook although it wasn't on the menu, because pizza was Julie's favorite. As they lingered over coffee, Dan lit a Cuban cigar he'd bought at the front desk. Julie made a half-hearted attempt to grab it and reminded him that the doctors had warned him against smoking. Well, he hadn't been smoking, he said, and besides, he wasn't going to inhale.

Back in their room, Dan made airplane reservations for the next day, and Julie began packing. Dan longed to sleep in his own bed, to be a little closer to his doctor and pharmacy, and to have lunch with a couple of his old friends, but he had grown used to this room, to the sounds Lisa made in the morning, to the sight of his daughter at the window tending the baby and eating her cereal. As he folded his clothes, he said, "Susan, come here. I need some help." He stood upright and looked at his daughter standing over the crib. He had called her Susan. She was feisty like her mother and not at all afraid to speak her mind.

"Julie," he said more loudly, "please come here. I need help in putting all this junk in my suitcase."

"That's right, Dad. You always used that helpless routine, and it always worked. Mother would pack your bag." This time his daughter did it.

Luis got them to the airport by six the next morning, four hours before the plane left, so they'd have enough time for security measures. Besides the metal detector for the passengers, the bags went through an x-ray machine three times, and they were frisked by guards. They had to take Lisa's emigration papers to three different cubicles for the various bureaucrats' approval. In the airport waiting room a guard brought a leashed German shepherd for a final check of everyone's bags. The dog stopped in front of Julie and nosed her suitcase and then the baby's diaper bag. The guard shouted something in Spanish, and two others came running. Dan stepped between his daughter and the guards. His heart was racing but he stood still. When one of the guards opened the diaper bag, the dog barked wildly at the baby's formula.

Once they were on the plane, Dan's heart slowed down, and his breathing eased. When they were in the air, his hands stopped sweating and he ordered a split of wine. Julie was asleep in the seat next to the window. He took a long drink and raised the glass in his second, private toast. This time his new granddaughter was soundly sleeping in the seat next to him.

A Matter of Trust

. . . .

*T*ED WAS rummaging in the refrigerator for a can of Budweiser. It was Friday after a tough week. On Monday, he'd started a new job as the editor, reporter, and photographer for a quarterly law enforcement magazine. The job paid only six hundred dollars a week and had very limited medical coverage, but he'd been out of work for almost six months after his copywriting job had been eliminated at the small advertising agency where he had worked for twenty years. They had told him that they were sorry and that he was doing good work, but the agency had lost two of its major clients, including the motorcycle company for which Ted had written ads.

For a while he had thought he would soon find another copywriting job, but he was fifty-one years old and as he kept hearing, "overqualified." God, he'd thought, if he heard that one more time, he'd come over the top of the desk and strangle some young personnel manager. But he kept going from interview to interview, wondering whether his tie was too wide or his lapels too narrow. He and Sally and the two kids had been living on his monthly unemployment check and the hundred and fifty dollars she was paid each week for her part-time job at the neighborhood drugstore.

Ted slumped in a chair in front of the television set in the living room. Sally was at work, and the kids had gone to the high school football game. He was relieved because he didn't feel like talking. Life had become a damn disappointment. His marriage was good, and he loved Sally and the kids, but he had little to show for a lifetime of hard work, of sixty-hour weeks, a two-pack-a-day cigarette habit, and a nervous stomach from too many deadlines. There wasn't a dime saved for the kids' college. He hadn't taken a vacation in five years. Last month, for the first time in his life, he had received several dunning letters from creditors. And he still couldn't shake off the humiliation of standing in the unemployment line at the county welfare office.

He took a long, cold swallow of beer and turned on the television. Dan Rather was going over the day's headline stories. Ted watched a story about flooding along the Mississippi River and a feature about the explosion of country music halls in Branson, Missouri. The lead-in to a Congressional debate over a proposed extension of unemployment benefits caught his attention, and he turned up the volume. The story began with a shot of people standing in front of an employment office in Chicago. A gray-haired man in his late fifties described his struggle trying to find work and said he didn't know what he'd do when his unemployment checks stopped.

The story shifted to the floor of the House where a smartly dressed Congressman from the Midwest was railing against the bill. "Quite simply," he said, "we can't afford it. Small business can't afford it. Main Street can't afford it. The taxpayers can't afford it. But more than that, we shouldn't pad a government dole that's already being abused. Too many people are using unemployment benefits to avoid finding work. There are plenty of jobs out there. I don't want to spend one more dime until I'm assured that those people out of work really want to work. It's a matter of trust."

My God, Ted thought, that's Jack. They had been in grade school together. Jack had been one of Ted's best friends, but they hadn't seen each other in thirty years. Ted looked out the window at the sturdy old white oak in his backyard. Forty years ago he and Jack had played in the tree fort they'd built in a similar oak tree.

The tree fort had a two-piece ladder that they could pull up whenever they were in the mood for privacy. That was most of the time. Parents couldn't spy on you up there, girls couldn't overhear you up there, and little brothers couldn't climb up there, so it was a good place to keep your most secret stuff: a Swiss army knife, a Nellie Fox rookie card, a beat-up copy of *Playboy* found in a dumpster behind Lincoln School. Ted and Jack were in the tree fort the very hour that Fidel Castro announced he was Cuba's new leader. They'd been listening to a Cubs game on a portable radio when a network reporter broke in with a news bulletin. Jack already had an interest in politics. Ted barely knew where Cuba was, but Jack knew about Batista and his cozy relationships with American capitalists. Jack's dad was a Republican, and Ted's dad was a lifelong Democrat, in a county where no Democrat had been elected to office since the FDR landslide in 1932. Sometimes Ted wished his old man was a Republican like everybody else or at least not such an active Democrat.

Ted always felt a little ashamed when he compared his family to Jack's. Jack's dad owned the local men's clothing store, and they lived in a big split-level rambler in the new section at the edge of town. The fifteen-room house had a den, a game room, and a wrap-around deck out back. Ted lived in a sixty-year-old two-story house near the railroad depot. The house was nice enough, particularly since Ted and his dad took such good care of the lawn and garden, but the rooms were small, the wallpaper was old and faded,

and the basement was unfinished. His dad did, however, install a toilet in one corner so the boys didn't
have to run upstairs when they were playing Ping
Pong. Ted remembered how his dad used to come
down after his shift ended at the foundry, pull the cover
down on the crapper, sit there with a bottle of beer in
his hand and read the paper.

Ted was proud of his old man except when Jack was
around because Jack was so well-spoken, whereas
Ted's dad threw around slang and four-letter words
with relish. When the old man told Ted that Jack
was "a well-bred sissy," Ted hollered that Jack was just
polite.

Jack invited Ted to all his junior-high parties, where
the best-looking girls in school came to be seen. And
Jack had pulled Ted out of the deep end of the park
pool when he ran out of air, swallowed a quart of
water, and sank like a rock. Jack and Ted got good
grades in school. They were both good talkers and
related well to grown-ups. They vowed one day to
leave their hometown to pursue their dreams: Ted
would write a best-selling novel, and Jack just might
become president of the United States.

In high school their differences began to count
more. One afternoon Ted was in the backyard, sanding
down a rusty iron pipe that his father planned to use
for a rooftop television antenna. Ted's mother had
cleaned the dust and cobwebs off, Ted was to sand and
paint it, and his father would install it on the roof. No
longer would they be the only family on the block

without a television set. Ted was almost ready to apply the first coat of aluminum paint, when Jack rode up on his brand-new three-speed bicycle. Proudly Ted told him they were about to buy a television and hook it up as soon as his dad got the antenna on the roof. Jack looked puzzled as he walked around the pipe resting on a pair of sawhorses.

"Why don't you just hire one of those antenna services?" Jack asked. "Then you wouldn't have to spend all that time painting a grungy old pipe."

"Because some of us aren't rich like you are," he blurted out. "Some of us have to work for what we want."

Jack got on his new bike and rode off.

It was a week before the boys talked again. They got together to study once in a while, and they both had roles in the junior-class play but Ted no longer shared his secrets with Jack. He found other friends, whose fathers didn't belong to the country club or own their own businesses.

Then one day Jack stopped him in the hallway at high school and asked if he could help in Ted's campaign for class president. Jack had run for the position but had been eliminated in the primary election, and now the race was down to Ted and Mike Molina, the quarterback on the football team. Ted invited Jack to come over to his house on Thursday, when he and three other friends were going to work on his speech for the Friday assembly.

When Jack arrived, Ted and his friends were in the

basement with an old Royal typewriter and papers spread out on the Ping Pong table. They played Ping Pong and pieced together a ten-minute speech. At nine o'clock, after they had consumed two bags of potato chips and half a case of Coke, Ted typed in his three-finger style the five-page speech.

"I'm honored to be here as a candidate for class president," it began. "My opponent is a worthy one, who cares deeply about this school. But this is more than a popularity contest. It is about which of us has the best vision for what this class ought to do and what kind of legacy it ought to leave for the classes that follow. Let me tell you about the vision I have." The speech then outlined a tutoring project, a fund-raiser for lights on the tennis court, and a plan allowing the student council to advise the administration about the curriculum. After Ted read it to the assembled group, Jack said he had to leave to finish a book report, but he took the carbon copy of the speech with him to see if he could make any last-minute improvements. The others stayed for more Coke and Ping Pong.

The next morning Ted was at school early. There'd be three hundred seniors at the nine o'clock assembly, and he wanted to sound and look good, even though he hadn't slept very well. Jack met him at his locker. "Good news," he said. "The kids on the assembly committee said Mike's agreed that you could give your speech last. He's nervous, and he wants to get his speech over with. You get to have the last word."

As Ted sat on the stage in the gymnasium, he was comforted to see his three speech-writing buddies in the front row. They gave him a thumbs-up. Jack was nowhere in sight. Then the principal stepped up to the microphone and introduced Mike Molina. The applause was loud as Mike strode forward, tall and handsome in his blazer and khaki slacks.

"I'm honored to be here as a candidate for class president," he began. "My opponent is a worthy one, who cares deeply about this school. But this is more than a popularity contest. It is about which of us has the best vision for what this class ought to do and what kind of legacy it ought to leave for the classes that follow." Mike glanced over at Ted and smiled as he continued his speech.

When it was his turn, Ted stumbled to the podium and stammered through an impromptu speech studded with the phrase "Like my opponent, I also . . ."

Afterward Ted waited for Mike Molina backstage. Mike, smiling, wished him luck.

"Luck, my ass," Ted hollered. "Where did you get your speech?"

"I wrote most of it this morning before school. Jack came over to my house and had a lot of good ideas, and he knew how to put them in words. What do you want to know for?"

"Forget it. My bitch is with Jack."

Ted found Jack walking out of his chemistry class. He pushed him back into the empty classroom. Tears began to stream down Ted's face. He couldn't stop them. He pounded Jack on the chest and screamed, "You bastard, you dirty bastard. We were friends. And you gave him my speech."

Jack just stood there with his eyes on the floor.

"Why did you do it? Tell me why, you bastard."

Still Jack said nothing. Ted started to walk away.

"I don't know why I did it," Jack said. "It was a joke, that's all. It was just a joke."

Ted came back to the doorway and looked at Jack standing against the blackboard. He wanted to say something, but the words weren't there. He turned and stomped away.

Ted lost the election. He put Jack number one on his shit list. Being class president didn't turn out to be much of a job for Mike, and Ted had plenty of friends who played in the band, met for hamburgers at the corner restaurant, and drank beer from quart bottles in the back seat of a '57 Chevy on Saturday nights. The last time Ted saw Jack was graduation day.

Ted had hardly thought of Jack in the past thirty years, but now seeing him on the news brought everything back in excruciating detail.

When Sally got home, she looked tired. These days there were streaks of gray in her chestnut brown hair and circles under her eyes.

"Anything on the news tonight, honey?" she asked.

"There was a story on extending unemployment benefits, and they had some Congressman ranting against it."

"What did he say?"

"Something about a matter of trust—you know, the same old bullshit."

Ted heaved himself out of his chair and headed for the kitchen for another beer.

He Came Alone This Year

. . . .

*I*T WAS A perfect setting for writing a short story: a cozy log cabin, a window with a view of Lake Superior, a pale pink sky at sunset, and tiny Spruce Creek tumbling into the lake. I could hear the soft whine of my new laptop computer with its blinking cursor, eager to respond to a tap on the keyboard. But I couldn't get started. The ideas flitting through my mind on the way up to the North Shore were gone, and I was staring at the little red cabin at the mouth of the creek.

My wife came over and put her chin on my shoulder. "There's that same station wagon in front of the cabin," Kris said. "That's the family with the two kids."

For the last four years this family had come the same week: two kids in their early teens, their mother who looked like Joanne Woodward, and the husband and father, a middle-aged guy with a round face, white hair, and a crisp press to his shirt and jeans.

The next morning was bright and clear and cool, with a gentle wind out of the north. The lake was robin's egg blue. From the window I could see the color of the pebbles and stones on the bottom of the bay near the mouth of the creek. The shades of the red cabin were still drawn, and there wasn't a sign of life. That's funny, I thought—usually the kids are out running around. And the family couldn't have gone to Grand Marais because the car was still there.

I was eating oatmeal and raisins when Kris returned from her morning jog. "I found out why we haven't seen the family over at that cabin," she said. "The reason is that there's no family there. I ran into the cabin caretaker and she said they got divorced and he came alone this year."

I sat at the keyboard and began typing. When I looked up, I saw the man come out of the cabin. He looked a little heavier, and his face seemed more creased. He was carrying a pair of chest waders, a fly rod, and a tackle box. He sat on the top step and leaned back against the railing. He let the waders slide down the steps and plopped a foot in and then the other. He stood up and shimmied into the rubber casing. He took a long time adjusting the waders before he pulled the suspenders up over his shoulders. He sat down again and assembled the fly rod. It was a three-piecer, a bamboo antique. He touched his brow and then gently rubbed the end of a section before inserting it into the other. He was using some of his skin's natural oil to lubricate the couplings. He sighted down the assembled rod to make sure the rod guides were aligned. He pulled a lime-green fly line through the guides. He put on a pair of wire-rimmed glasses from his shirt pocket and tied the tippet, or leader, to the fly line. Then he sorted through his tackle box, chose a fly so tiny that I couldn't see it, and affixed it to the leader. He secured the hook in the cork handle, stood up on the steps, and waved the rod back and forth several times. He sat down again, held his rod upright, and stared out over Lake Superior.

When the hell was he going fishing?

A few minutes later he set the fly rod against the railing, unhooked his suspenders, and pulled off the waders. He snipped the fly off the leader and wound the line back onto the reel. He disassembled the rod and took the whole shooting match back in the cabin. He shut the door, and I didn't see him for the rest of the day.

I didn't tell my wife about this strange scene, and as I was going to bed, I vowed to quit watching the guy. I went to sleep with the patter of a gentle but steady rain on the roof.

The next day the sun was out, the big lake was an inviting blue, and there was just enough breeze to take the sweat off my forehead. We walked about three miles before breakfast, a heart-healthy combination of cereal, toast, and fresh cantaloupe. I took my coffee to the computer keyboard. There he was again, sitting on the ground about ten yards from his cabin door.

He was digging dandelions with a pocket knife. He'd stick the knife in the ground, give it a little shove, pull up the dandelion, shake the dirt from the roots, and toss it on a pile at his feet. This was no manicured lawn he was working on. This was Canadian Shield, granite covered by a couple of inches of topsoil. He kept weeding for most of the morning, gradually moving around to the other side of the cabin.

Maybe he was going to make dandelion wine, I thought, but probably he only wanted some mindless task to take him from breakfast to lunch. I had known times when just getting through the day was a victory. My own divorce after a brief marriage had been painful enough, and this neighbor must have been married for some twenty years, and he had a couple of kids.

Early that afternoon he carried a laundry bag out to his car, tossed it in the back seat, stood and looked at the lake for a while before driving off. It was well after supper time when he came back. He must have gone to the laundromat in Grand Marais. He had a neat little stack of underwear, socks, and shirts.

For the next two days, I forced myself not to watch him, and Kris and I hiked and talked and read. I'd even managed to finish one story and make a respectable start on another. On our last night we drove into Grand Marais for supper. The town was nearly deserted, and we held hands as we walked down the street, feeling a little sad that our week was ending.

Afterward, about an hour before dusk, I did a little fishing, just casting from shore at the mouth of Spruce Creek. Because of the nightly rain that week, the creek was running high, brown, and dirty. But Superior was blue, with a golden haze on the horizon and a little chill and dampness in the air, as I cast an orange spoon into the lake. I'd never caught a fish from Lake Superior and I didn't expect to on this night, but I enjoyed fishing anyway, sailing the spoon out into the river's vanishing current in the lake, pumping the rod, and letting the lure flutter and fall.

Suddenly the spoon stopped, and the rod bent. I set the hook. I had a fish. I let out a whoop. I eased the fish toward the shore to beach her.

Ten yards in front of me, the water exploded, as a silver torpedo leaped a foot into the air. I kept pumping the rod, bringing her closer. She leaped again.

As I slid her onto the shore, I estimated she was eight or nine pounds. She was a dark iridescent green with black spots on her back and a bright red slash down her side: a steelhead, a rainbow trout that lived in the lake and returned to the river to spawn. It was the first steelhead I'd ever caught, and I was tempted to keep her, at least long enough to show my wife, but the fish wouldn't survive a trip up to the cabin. I unhooked the steelhead and gently slid her back into the lake.

When I scrambled up to the top of the bank, our neighbor was standing on his porch.

"That was quite a fish," he said. "I saw the whole thing."

"That's good," I said. "So I have a witness in case my wife doubts me."

He laughed. He had a handsome face, when a smile creased it. "What did you use for a lure?" he asked.

I showed him the orange spoon.

"I brought along my spinning rod," he said. "I figured I'd do some shore casting."

I unhooked the lure and held it out. "Take this," I

said. "I've already caught my fish on it." At first he said no, of course, but I kept offering, and finally he took it.

"Thanks," he said. "I've got a couple of days left up here. I guess I'll fish the creek mouth in the morning."

The next morning was beautiful. We paid the bill and packed the car. As I was about to turn onto the highway for home, I remembered. I stopped the car.

I stood on the bank and looked down at the bay and Spruce Creek. The shore was deserted. The red cabin's door was closed, and the shades were pulled.

Maybe next year.

Way Beyond Journalism School

. . . .

I WAS BANGING away at the keyboard of the old Smith-Corona typewriter in the cluttered and stuffy newspaper office in the bowels of police headquarters when the radio speaker on the wall crackled: "Officer down. Officer down." I stopped typing. I swung around in my chair to face the radio. There were several moments of static followed by an almost plaintive plea: "Officer needs assistance. Shots fired. Officer needs assistance at Twenty-fourth and Lyndale Avenue North. Any squads in the area please respond."

Turning back to the typewriter, I ripped out the backgrounder I'd been working on, about a dramatic increase in neighborhood burglaries, and rolled in a fresh sheet of paper. The radio crackled to life again. Three squads were on the way, and I could hear their sirens in the background as the officers gave the dispatcher a breathless account of their progress to the scene.

It was eleven o'clock, so I had only three hours to put this story together before the afternoon final edition went to press. I was a three-month rookie, and I hadn't had a breaking story like this. I was off to a fast start as the paper's cop reporter. Just the day before, the city editor had dropped by the Rat Pit, the police newsroom, to tell me he was satisfied with the job I'd been doing, so I felt pretty cocky. I was finding a few good sources, I was learning to write faster, and I was developing a story list. I also knew that the name of the game in the newspaper business was What Have You Done For Me Lately.

I took the notes I'd typed from the radio dispatches and ran down the marble corridor to the homicide office, where a half-dozen detectives were milling around a city map on the wall. I walked past them to a corner desk where Joe was sitting with a telephone receiver cradled between his shoulder and ear, a kitchen match in one hand, and his pipe in the other. He struck the match on the desk top and lit up. He took a couple of short puffs and then inhaled deeply.

Joe was a veteran homicide cop who was one of my best sources. He was enough of a hot dog to like publicity and enough of a father to take an interest in a kid half his age. Joe had introduced me to the denizens of a world new to me: a hooker named Mona Lisa, a bookie named Legs, and a transvestite partial to purple lipstick and eye shadow. This cross-dresser called him Honey and was referred to by Joe as "the loveliest lady on the avenue." Joe himself looked as if he had walked out of the pages of *Esquire*, in his white shirt with French cuffs and sharply pressed pinstripe suit that fitted perfectly on his slim, tall frame, maybe six-four or six-five. His suit never seemed to wrinkle although he never took off his coat. He always wore a bow tie, suspenders, and highly shined wing tips, with silk socks. His colleagues wore polyester sport coats and clip-on ties. Joe looked like he belonged in a corporate boardroom, giving eager directors the latest on third-quarter earnings. But he was the best homicide detective west of New York City.

As soon as he hung up the phone, I asked him what was happening.

"We got a dead cop, kid," he said. "He was a rookie stopping a speeder. As he came up on the car, the guy pulled out a gun and shot him right in the belly. He died in the street." Joe paused. "Asshole. I want a piece of that frigging asshole."

The shooter, Joe said, was a convicted burglar in his twenties—the rookie cop had called in for a license check before approaching the car. So they had the suspect's name and description, but they didn't have him. According to a witness, he'd taken off running after firing two shots from a handgun. I thanked Joe for the information and sprinted down the hall, just about sliding past the door to my office. Leather soles and marble floors were a bad combination, and I'd almost fallen on my fanny a half dozen times as I raced down the hallway to call rewrite and make a deadline.

As I waited for Larry, the rewrite man, I felt proud of myself. I had the name of the victim. I knew how the shooting had happened. I had a description of the suspect. And I had enough of the chatter from the police radio to describe the hunt for the shooter. I dictated seven or eight paragraphs to Larry, who said he'd hold the story and wait for my update in half an hour. I looked in the reverse street directory for names and phone numbers of several residents near the shooting site. On my third phone call I reached a woman who had heard the two gunshots and had seen a man waving a revolver and running north on Lyndale, right past her living-room window.

I was flipping through my notebook, about to start typing, when I heard voices at the entrance to the office. My desk was tucked behind three old green wall lockers for coats and overshoes. The door of one of those lockers had a ragged hole the size of a half-dollar. The story was that a detective had been showing a young female reporter his .357 magnum revolver when her hand brushed his thigh and his finger brushed the trigger. You could throw a baseball through the hole in the back of the locker, which my desk was facing.

I was about to get up and see who was in the office when I heard Joe's voice. He was talking to several patrolmen. "I want you to listen up," he said. "I know where this asshole is. I just got a call from one of my snitches. He said this asshole is hiding in a blue and white cracker-box house on Knox Avenue North." Joe gave them the address. He was talking in short, quick bursts, barely raising his voice above a whisper. "Now this is important," he said. "I'm going to hit the front door, and this asshole is going to run to the back door, sure as hell. The back door comes out onto a yard and the alley, and there're about a dozen garages he could hide in or find a car." Joe told the patrolmen he wanted them positioned on the sides of the garage facing the back door. He wanted them armed with shotguns. "When he comes out that back door, and he will, kill the son of a bitch. You hear me? Kill the son of a bitch."

The patrolmen mumbled their acknowledgments as they left the room. I went out and found Joe pausing to light his pipe. We were alone in the hall.

"Joe, I was in the office when you talked to the cops. I heard what you said."

He took the pipe from his mouth and looked me straight in the eye. "Yeah, what about it?"

"Well, I mean, I mean . . . I heard you talk about wanting to kill this guy. You can't be serious."

"Look, kid, this is not some college game we're playing. This asshole killed a cop. Now unless you're going to try and stop me, get the hell out of the way and go back to your typewriter."

He turned and strode down the hall. I stumbled back to my office and slumped in my chair. I didn't know what to do. I couldn't sit around, so I got up and wandered down the hall. I saw the sign for the chief's office. That's it, I thought. I'll go in and say something about the shooting and the suspect and the need for plenty of officers to go out and pick him up. If there are twenty cops out there, I reasoned, it'll be harder for two of them to blow anyone away.

Still uncertain, I stood outside the chief's office for a few minutes. I didn't like the chief. He always had a smirk on his face, and he talked in circles. I poked my head in his door. He nodded, so I went in and stood nervously in front of his desk.

"Chief, I'm covering this story about the cop shooting, and I hear the suspect is cornered on the Northside. I just wondered whether you were going to send a lot of squads out there since the suspect is armed?"

"We've got the situation under control. I believe you know Joe from homicide. Well, he's handling the whole thing. Any other questions?"

I went back to the press room and put on my coat and walked to my car in the lot across the street. I pulled out, turned onto Fifth Street and headed toward the Northside. I was angry and my hands were shaking on the steering wheel. I'd taken a dozen journalism courses in college, taught by men with Ph.D.'s who'd written textbooks on reporting, and not one had ever said anything about a mess like this. I rolled down the window and let a blast of crisp November air cool my face. I took a long, deep breath and pressed on the accelerator.

Five minutes later I was at Twenty-fourth and Lyndale, and there wasn't a squad car in sight. Now, where in the hell was the suspect hiding? It was a blue and white house, but I couldn't remember the street. For the next half hour I drove up and down alleys, careening around corners and bumping over curbs. It was useless. I pulled over and put my head on the steering wheel. After a while I lifted my head and looked down the street. A block up, on the corner, was a small church. I drove there.

The white clapboard church was badly in need of a

coat of paint, and the brown wooden cross above the door seemed about to fall. I hesitated for a minute and walked in. The sanctuary was cold and dark and smelled musty. There was a stack of bulletins on a table, and I picked one up. This was a Baptist church, a black church, and Pastor Robinson would be preaching next Sunday on "The Power of Prayer." At the altar rail in front of the pulpit I knelt on the threadbare carpet. I folded my hands on the rail and looked up at the tiny stained-glass window. I hadn't been in church for two years. "Our Father," I began, "Who art in heaven." When I finished, I added a few words of my own: "God, please don't let them shoot anybody. Thank you."

When I turned to leave, I saw an old lady sitting in the second pew. Her shopping bag was in the aisle beside her. As I walked past, she reached out for my arm and pulled it toward her. "Son," she said, "I don't know what your trouble is. But we've all got it, you know?" She patted my hand. "With a young fella like you," she said, "you'll get what you need." I thanked her and drove back to the police station.

I was hanging up my coat in the old locker with the bullet hole, when I heard a commotion in the hall. Half a dozen patrolmen were scurrying down the hall, and at the front of the pack was Joe, wearing a camel's-hair topcoat with every gray hair on his head still in place. They were hustling along the suspect with his hands cuffed behind his back and a brown jacket draped over the back of his head. He was young and stocky and had

shoulder-length blond hair. He looked dazed, and his lips were locked in a grimace. Then I noticed a welt at the corner of his mouth and a trickle of blood on his chin. The group crowded onto the jail elevator.

I hurried to the homicide office and waited there until the captain got a phone call from the booking desk and gave me the details of the arrest. Back in the press office, I quickly typed an insert for my story and called rewrite.

"Police arrested a 28-year-old suspect about an hour after the shooting. He was hiding in a house in the 2900 block of Knox Avenue North. Detectives said that his car was parked in a garage behind the house and that he surrendered without a scuffle. He was taken to police headquarters for booking into the Hennepin County Jail.

"Police discovered the whereabouts of the suspect after receiving a phone call from an informant. He was arrested by two uniformed patrolmen as he attempted to flee out the back door of the house. The officers said he was not armed. They are still searching for the murder weapon.

"Police administrators hailed the arrest as a 'fine piece of police work that the community can be proud of.'"

When I finished dictating the story to Larry, the city editor got on the phone. "Congratulations," he said. "You got the story, and we'll get it in the final edition."

After I hung up, I leaned back in the chair, closed my eyes, and folded my arms across my chest. My shirt was soaked with sweat, and I was exhausted.

"Kid, you got a minute?" I lifted my head and saw

Joe standing there. It was an effort to look him in the eye. "I just wanted to get something straight," he said. "That business in your office earlier, well, that was a lot of hot-air woofing from an old cop. Sometimes in the heat of battle . . . well, you know."

I nodded, and he walked away. I sat upright in my chair and stared straight ahead. Suddenly I felt like a rookie again.

Have Mercy on Us

. . . .

I PUT MY key in the lock of the third-floor apartment, balancing a sack of groceries on my knee as I tried to open the door. The phone was ringing. "Just hold on a goddamn minute," I muttered under my breath. "I'm coming, I'm coming."

It was Stan on the phone. We hadn't seen each other for a year, since I'd taken a job as a rookie newspaper reporter in Minneapolis and he'd wound up at Fort Benning, Georgia, for his officer's basic training.

"I'm heading over to Nam," he said, matter-of-factly, "and I want to drive up and see you before I go. Maybe you can store a few of my things." He'd arrive early on Saturday morning. I said I'd have a cold beer waiting for him and I'd leave the front door unlocked.

I hung up the phone and put away the groceries, TV dinners and cans of chili. I sat down at the kitchen table and lit a cigarette and opened a bottle of Budweiser. Damn, old Stan is going to Vietnam. It was 1965, and the casualty list was still small, but the risks were growing larger and larger. Every morning the radio news gave the latest body counts.

Stan was my best friend. We'd been buddies since the eighth grade. We smoked our first cigarettes together on a Boy Scout camping trip when we were twelve. We drank our first beers together when we were fourteen. I stole a couple of dusty bottles of Chief Oshkosh from an old case in my grandmother's basement. We smuggled them in a sleeping bag to a friend's cabin and sat on the end of the dock, sipping and talking under the stars on a warm June night, as we waited for that head-spinning rush our older friends had described.

"Do you feel anything?" I asked.

Stan said he thought he might be getting dizzy. We giggled. Then we laughed out loud.

"Shit," Stan said, "I've felt higher smoking a Winston."

The beer was flat and stale, but Stan and I felt the close connection of boys sharing adventures, testing parental limits, or breaking the speed laws in a '57 Oldsmobile. And when my mother was dying of cancer while we were in college, Stan had helped me hold her hand as the chemotherapy took its toll. He was with me when the doctors told me her chances were slim to none, and he walked with me on the way home from the hospital as I alternately cried and hollered over the damn unfairness of it all.

I got home late Friday night, a little wobbly from one too many beers after work with a couple of the other young reporters. We'd been bitching about schedules and editors and wondering about our futures. But as I stripped off my necktie and peeled off my shirt, I was smiling. I was off to a good start on a job I wanted. I was going to spend the weekend with my old friend. And I wasn't the one going to Vietnam. The last thing I did before I crashed was to unlock my apartment door.

The next thing I remember was something wet on my face. I slapped at my nose, opened my eyes, saw a strange dog, and heard Stan cackle.

"I see you've met Major," he said.

I scratched the beagle behind the ears. "Jesus, boy," I said, "you're an old dog, gray around the muzzle. Are you the best he could find?" Major wagged his tail and took a swipe at my nose with his tongue.

Stan was in the bedroom doorway, holding a couple of long-necked bottles of Pabst he'd brought with him. He offered me one. I struggled to my feet and asked for a cup of coffee instead.

By the time I got awake, Stan had already rummaged through the almost empty refrigerator and was scrambling the last of the eggs. "Dammit," he said, "you don't even have any onion to put in these eggs. I don't suppose you have any Tabasco sauce?" I found a little bottle in the cupboard. Stan shook out a teaspoonful or two, stirred the eggs one more time, and emptied the frying pan onto a couple of plates.

As we ate, we talked about old times and new experiences. When I asked how he felt about going to Vietnam, he just shrugged. "It's not like I got a hell of a lot of choice," he said. "I guess I'm as ready as I'm going to be." I asked him what he'd heard about Nam, what he thought it would be like, whether he was scared. Like me, he'd never killed anything except fish. He admitted he was uneasy over the idea of combat, but it was clear he didn't want to talk much about it.

After breakfast Stan brought in some belongings for me to store: a guitar, his beer-mug collection from college, a tennis racquet, a half-dozen rods and reels, and a tackle box. As we were putting the stuff in my storage locker in the basement, Stan said, "I was wondering what to do about Major. I don't know who to leave the dog with. I don't suppose you got the time or the . . ." He let the sentence trail away.

"Shit, you know I'd love to take the dog, Stan, but this work schedule of mine doesn't make it possible. I'm gone all day, and there's no place to tie the dog."

"I understand. I shouldn't have asked. Anyway, the dog has a touch of arthritis, and it takes him a while to get going in the morning. He probably wouldn't have been able to climb the stairs up to your apartment in six months."

"I'll find a home for your dog."

"That's okay. Forget it."

We finished storing his belongings, put the dog in Stan's car with us and had lunch at McDonald's. We ate our burgers in silence. Then we talked a little about the Twins, and Stan lamented the fact that he'd miss most of the baseball season. He was going to be a long way from peaceful summer nights and upper deck seats and cold beer. I was trying to imagine what he'd be confronting. What would the country look like? How do they fight these wars? Do you see your enemy? Could he kill somebody? Jesus, I thought, I'd be scared all the time, scared shitless.

"Let's take a ride out in the country," Stan said, "someplace with some woods and water." I hadn't had much time off to explore the countryside, but I knew of a pretty stand of white pines near the Saint Croix River north of town.

As Stan drove north on Highway 8 past fields and farms, the sky was blue, the breeze was warm, and the countryside was a pastel green. It was a bluebird June day. Stan turned on the radio to a station playing a Kingston Trio song. We'd spent many a night at college in student saloons, drinking beer by the pitcher and plugging the jukebox to hear "Scotch and Soda" or "Tom Dooley." Pretty soon we were both singing along, even trying to harmonize. It wasn't good, but it was loud and energetic: "It takes a worried man to sing a worried song. I'm worried now, but I won't be worried long."

For the next half hour we recalled stories of our partying and carousing, of the women we met and those we never did find the courage to ask for a date. "Remember the time," Stan said, "that you took the dance lessons, and I caught you practicing with Bill? Jeez, you guys were a pair. He was at least a foot taller than you, and you guys never could decide who was going to lead." I reminded him of the time when he was in ROTC and worried about his squeaky voice, hardly authoritative for shouting marching commands. One of his company commanders suggested he chew tobacco for a couple of weeks. I came home one night to find him throwing up in the john.

We crossed the river into Saint Croix Falls, and I told him to turn off onto a gravel county road north of town. We laid down a cloud of dust as Stan eased the car between chuck holes and straddled the shoulder and the crown that could easily have ripped off the muffler.

"Some road," he grunted.

"You said you wanted to get out in the country." We pulled to a stop at a turnaround next to a little creek that seemed to tumble out of an opening in an alder thicket. There was a path into the woods. Stan put Major on his leash. He pulled a pack of Winstons from his shirt pocket and lit a cigarette with the Zippo he'd had since we were freshmen in college.

"Old buddy, I've got to deal with my dog," he said. "I'm going to put him down. It's the only way."

"No, it's not the only way. Let me handle it. I know a couple of guys with families who'd probably be glad to have a dog for their kids."

"Major isn't all that good with kids. He's got a little ornery ever since somebody pulled his ears or grabbed his tail or something. He's an old man, kind of set in his ways."

"Then, I'll take him to a vet, and he could give him a shot."

Stan put his arm on my shoulder. "This is my dog and I've got to do it myself. You can stay here."

Stan opened the car trunk and took out a forty-five caliber automatic in a black holster. He handed me the leash while he rummaged around and found a clip. I heard the click of the clip snapping into place. He took out an entrenching tool, a small collapsible army shovel, and we headed down the path into the woods, with the lacy boughs of the white pines towering over us. We walked in silence with Major following along at my heel. For a moment I thought of unhooking the leash and telling the dog to scat. But he wouldn't have run. He was too old to run, and Stan was his best friend.

When we got to the top of a little rise overlooking the creek, Stan stopped. He turned around to look at me and the dog. There were tears in his eyes. "Give me the leash," he said. He tied it to a small birch. He took the forty-five out of the holster. His hand was shaking as he bent over and put the muzzle behind the dog's ear. He moved between me and Major, and I heard the sharp crack. Stan turned, facing me. Tears were streaming down his face.

Major lay on the ground, blood oozing from the hole in his skull. One of his front paws twitched. I ran into the brush and found a fallen oak limb and rushed back and swung at Major's head. The bough landed with a dull thud. He was dead.

I turned to Stan and put my arms around him. I could feel his tears against my neck. We were both shaking. We held each other so long and so tightly I could hardly breathe. Then Stan picked up the shovel and began digging next to the birch, throwing pine needles, leaves, and dirt this way and that. I used the shovel to even up the sides of the small grave while Stan went back to the car to get Major's blanket. He lifted the dog's body and placed it on the blanket, and we lowered Major into the grave. Stan covered the body with a mound of dirt and gently tamped it down with the shovel blade.

"Maybe you could say a prayer," he said.

"God," I prayed, "I hope you can receive Major, here, into your care. He was a good dog and a good companion to my best friend, who loved him. And God, please take care of us and have mercy on us. Amen."

We walked back to the car and drove silently down the gravel road. My mind kept racing for something to say, for some way to make sense of what we'd just

done. But no words, no sentences would take shape. As we came into Saint Croix Falls, I said, "Let's get a six-pack. I could use a beer." Stan stopped at a bar and came back with a six-pack of bottles of Pabst. I found a church key in the glove box and opened a couple of bottles as we pulled out of town. Stan turned on the radio. They were playing "Unchained Melody." It reminded me of our senior prom, when Stan and I had doubled, Stan with Mary and me with Bev, a million years ago.

I took the Pabst from between my legs, took a long pull, and put a foot up on the dashboard. Then I saw the spots of blood, still red, on my jeans.

You Missed a Spot

. . . .

*I*T WAS seventeen blocks from Ted's father's old house to Grand Meadows, the nursing home where he now lived. Driving there one spring morning, Ted saw every backyard in need of mowing, every house in need of painting, and every pothole in need of filling. He'd driven three hundred miles, but he was in no hurry to see the old man. They told him this was the best place in town. Where they got the name Grand Meadows he couldn't imagine. There was nothing grand about the gray one-story cement-block building, and there hadn't been a meadow for at least fifty years.

When Ted turned into the driveway of Grand Meadows, he said a short prayer that his father would recognize him. The last time his father hadn't known him. He just sat in his wheelchair, staring into space, until he suddenly announced, "I got to take a piss."

There was a bedpan on his night table. Ted took it to him and started to pull down his sweatpants. His father was wearing a diaper. Ted couldn't bring himself to unpin the thing and hold his old man's penis.

"Dad," he said, "I'm going to get the nurse. She'll help you."

Ted ran up and down the hall but couldn't find a nurse. By the time he got back to the room, a dark wet spot was spreading in the crotch of his father's sweat pants.

"I'm sorry, Dad. I should have helped you. I just . . ." He couldn't think of a way to say it. His father didn't speak. He didn't look at him.

This visit had to be better, Ted thought, as he walked down the hall. The ammonia smell in the hallway was almost enough to knock him over. Obviously his father wasn't the only one peeing in his pants. Ted recalled the joke he'd heard from a nurse on his last visit: What's sixty feet long and smells like urine? A line dance at a nursing home. Yet this place was always clean, and they had a yellow cardboard tulip on his father's door. Ted stood in front of it, took a deep breath, knocked, and opened the door.

It was dark in the room, and his father was in bed. He had pillows under his head and buttocks and one wedged between his shoulder and the bars on the side of his bed. He was facing the wall with his knees pulled up to his chest. Ted walked around the bed and gently nudged his shoulder.

"Dad," he whispered, "it's your son. I've come to see you." His father opened his eyes. "Do you know who I am?"

"Of course I know you. You're my son," he said with a broad grin. This time his blue eyes were bright, focused, and engaged.

Ted gave him a hug. His body felt like a match-stick

mannequin, brittle and sharp edged. Ted knelt down beside the bed because his father couldn't lift his head off the pillow.

"Dad, you know what weekend this is? It's the fishing opener. There must be a million boats on the road today. Remember our fishing trips together?"

He nodded and slowly reached toward Ted's face, as if trying to pull him closer, and said, "Do you remember the trip to the Cisco Chain?"

That was in the September just before Ted started college. He and his father found a little lake with a boulder shoreline surrounded by towering Norway pines near the border of Wisconsin and Upper Michigan. They cast Dardevle lures toward the rocks and pulled in northern pike weighing three and four pounds. In half an hour they had their Wisconsin limit of northerns on their stringer. When a fisherman drifted by and asked how they were doing, Ted's father proudly held up the stringer.

"You look to be half a dozen northerns over your limit," the man said.

"No, we're all right," Ted's father said. "I have the Wisconsin fishing regulations right in my tackle box."

"The only trouble is," the fisherman replied, "you're in Michigan, not Wisconsin."

Ted's father didn't have a Michigan fishing license. He started the motor and hid the stringer of northerns under his old jacket in the bottom of the boat. It never seemed to cross his mind to release the fish.

Now Ted held his hand and said, "We were lucky we

didn't get pinched that day. They'd have confiscated our boat, motor, and fishing poles."

Ted felt his father's fingers tighten. His old hands were crippled with arthritis—the knuckles swollen, the fingers curled. Now he couldn't hold a fishing pole or a fork or even toilet paper.

On this morning at least his father was able to take pleasure in his memories. Most of the times he remembered were with him in a boat. He never talked about work or politics, which used to be so important to him.

"Yeah, son, we had some good times. I sure wish . . ." He paused and started to cry softly.

"Dad, you know I'd sure love to go fishing with you again."

Ted launched into a story about their friend and guide, Ben. He'd taken them to a bass lake in the Upper Peninsula where they'd caught a dozen fish. During a midday thunderstorm they pulled the canoe onto a small island to eat their soggy sandwiches and have a swig of coffee from the thermos. Ted's father was sitting with his back against a birch tree, a cup in his hand, and a cigarette in his mouth.

"Look," he said, "there's another damn fool out on this lake." A canoe floated by—only it was empty.

"I got a feeling I know who the damn fool is," Ben said, looking right at Ted, who was supposed to have secured the canoe up on shore.

Ben ran into the water and swam after the canoe. He grabbed one of the gunwales, rolling the canoe and throwing everything in it—rods, reels, and tackle boxes—into thirty feet of water. They built a fire, and Ben dried his clothes. Ted kept mumbling that he was sure he'd tied the damned thing up.

"That was the end of our fishing, wasn't it?" his father said, trying to raise his head off the pillow. "Yeah, and you kept asking Ben whether he was going to charge us for a whole day of fishing or just a half."

A nurse came in, hoisted his father out of bed, and plunked his ninety-eight pound body in a wheelchair. "Got to get them up," she said matter-of-factly, "or they tend to get pneumonia."

Ted began massaging a bony shoulder.

"I'm grateful, Dad, for everything you did for me. You've been a good father."

"I always tried my best for you."

"I know. You taught me to work hard, Dad. All my life I've known how to work hard, and it's got me noticed."

"All the men in our family knew the meaning of a good day's work."

"And you also taught me the meaning of a good day's fishing: peace and contentment. And I've come to admire your big-D Democrat politics. You used to say the trouble with rich folks is they think they're higher on the food chain than the rest of us."

"Hell," his father said, "those rich bastards don't even want the government to carry the mail."

Ted remembered the night his father took him to the train station to see Harry Truman on his "Give 'em Hell" whistle-stop tour across the country. Perched on the old man's shoulders, Ted was too young to understand political history, but he absorbed the idea that government could help ordinary people in need. He also absorbed his father's knack for making friends. One was thirty, and one was eighty-five. One was a bank president, and one was a janitor. One ran a sports shop in northern Wisconsin, and another was a chaplain at the state prison. He didn't forget birthdays, he listened to troubles, and he always had an extra ten spot for emergencies.

"Dad," Ted said, "you really taught me a lot. You did a good job, and I love you."

He cupped his father's face in his hands and kissed him on the cheek. Ted was proud of himself for telling his father of his gifts. He also wanted to know what the old man thought of him and the life he'd been living. But he was anxious, even a little frightened about asking.

When Ted was nine years old, his father asked him to paint the picket fence behind the garage. Its white paint was cracked and peeling and streaked with dirt. On the first day the temperature was ninety degrees, and Ted scraped, sanded, and brushed that fence for eight hours. His arms ached, the sweat stung his eyes, and he could hardly uncurl his fingers from the sandpaper block. By the time he finished sanding, it was almost dusk and his father still wasn't home.

The next day Ted was back at work by eight o'clock. He had a gallon of ivory paint and two brushes, a big brush for the sides of the slats and a little one for in between. His father had a steady hand and could stroke paint on the putty of a storm window without getting a speck on the pane. "It's a nice, easy motion," he'd say, "and the idea is to brush lightly. That way you don't leave streaks." All day Ted painted with his father's long, even brush strokes. He picked off the brush bristles left behind and repainted. He also got splotches of white paint on his jeans, T-shirt, tennis shoes, face, and arms.

When he walked into the kitchen, his mother shrieked, "Young man, you go right down to the basement and wash off with turpentine." When he came back upstairs, she asked him to show her the fence, and she oohed and aahed as he knew she would.

Around five-thirty his father's Chevrolet hardtop pulled into the driveway. Ted ran up and exclaimed, "I finished it, Dad! Come on and take a look."

His father walked up and down the length of the fence. He put his arm around Ted's shoulder and gave him a squeeze. "You did a pretty good job, son," he said, "but you missed a spot, right over here on the bottom of the last two slats." Ted said he'd fix it right now, but his father said, "Tomorrow will be soon enough. It's time for supper, and we've both had a long day." Silently they walked to the back door.

Now they sat silently in his father's room, side by side, chair to wheelchair.

"Dad, now that I'm fifty years old, there's something I'd like to know. I'd like to know what you think of me, you know, what kind of man I turned out to be."

"Well, I'm proud of you. You always got good grades in school, and you did well at work. You know I bragged about you to my friends."

He was staring straight ahead at the wall, so Ted moved around in front of him.

"I want to know, Dad, whether you think I'm a good man."

"Sure, you turned out fine." He paused. "The only thing I wish is that . . ." His voice faded away.

"Wish what, Dad?"

He didn't respond.

"Dad, you were talking about wishing I'd done something. What was it?"

After a while his father mumbled something about packing his bags and catching a plane.

"That's okay, Dad. We're in your room. There's no plane to catch."

His father seemed relieved. His eyes closed, and his head slumped against his chest. Ted wiped a trickle of saliva from the corner of his father's mouth, stroked the back of his head, and said goodbye. If he heard, he didn't acknowledge it.

The sun was out, and Ted looked at the swelling buds on the oak trees as he walked toward his car. At the far end of the parking lot an old apartment building was being remodeled, and a couple of young men in coveralls were on a scaffold painting the trim under the eaves. Ted looked up, and smiled. It's almost as if, he thought, he was checking to see if they'd missed a spot.

Scattering His Ashes

. . . .

*T*HE BLUE and white Cessna 150 was tethered to the end of the dock at the Crane Lake United States customs station, rocking gently back and forth on its aluminum pontoons. Scottie was waving to us as the Bear drove his rusty, old Pontiac station wagon into the gravel parking lot.

The Bear had organized this trip when he met Scottie at the spring sport show in Minneapolis. Scottie had started his flying service ten years ago and now had a fleet of five planes: two Cessnas, two Beavers, and a Twin Otter. The Bear, an outdoor writer for the paper, would meet people, light his pipe, whip out his notebook, and they'd tell him their life stories. They usually wound up inviting him on some sort of expedition, and on this trip Scottie was charging us only a hundred dollars, to cover the gas and oil. The September weather was perfect for our trip into Beaverhouse Lake that morning: the air was a crisp sixty degrees, and the birch had a tinge of yellow on their leaves. The mosquitoes and black flies were gone, so the Bear and I planned to pitch a tent near the Beaverhouse ranger station for our base camp while we explored two or three lakes in the Quetico looking for big smallmouth bass.

In ten minutes we loaded our gear onto the plane, the Bear in front and me in the back with our tent, sleeping bags, duffel bags, a full cooler, a box of food and our mess kits. I settled back against my duffel bag as Scottie took off from the customs shack. We idled out to the middle of the lake, and then Scottie revved the single engine, turned the nose into the wind, and roared down the watery runway. We bumped and bounced on the waves and jumped into the air. By the time we reached the end of the lake there were at least a hundred yards between the plane and the tops of the tallest pines. It was cramped, but I liked flying in bush planes, skimming over the tree tops and looking down on hundreds of lakes and rivers with waterfalls. I tried to pick out good fishing spots, where the water turned from the color of gin to the dark hue of a strong iced tea.

As the engine settled into a comfortable drone, Scottie said he thought the weather would be clear and warm for our three days. He advised us to hunt for the smallmouth at daybreak and dusk, searching the shallows with small surface baits. There was a boat at the ranger station we could use, and we had a three-horse Johnson, fuel-efficient so a tank of gas would last a week. In twenty minutes Scottie pointed to Beaverhouse Lake on the horizon. He reached under the pilot's seat for a small cardboard canister about as big as an economy-size salt container. "I meant to tell you guys before," he shouted, "but we've got a little mission before we land. This is some guy's ashes, and

his wife wants me to scatter them over Beaverhouse."
He handed the canister to the Bear, who handed it to
me. The cover on the top read, "Cremated Remains of
Tom Lobauer, 2-18-91." Scottie said, "Old Tom was a
regular to Quetico most of his life, and his wife wants
half his ashes scattered here, and the other half she's
going to scatter back home along the shore of Lake
Minnetonka." That was kind of amusing, I thought,
half here and half there, as if the guy couldn't make up
his mind where he belonged. But what the hell, they
were his ashes.

Scottie leveled the Cessna about a hundred yards
above the tamarack-colored water of Beaverhouse
Lake. I handed the canister to the Bear. Scottie tipped
the plane slightly and said, "Open the window and
shake out about half a can." As the Bear reached outside, a gust of wind blew the fine ashen contents all
over him, me, and our gear

"What the hell!" I hollered and wiped ash from my
lips.

"Is there any left in the can?" Scottie shouted. The
Bear shook his head. "Oh, Jesus," Scottie said. "His old
lady is expecting to scatter the other half of him in front
of their lake back home."

The Bear and I couldn't help laughing. We had
Tom's remains all over us, our sleeping bags, our field
jackets, even our fishing rods, as Scottie softly put
the Cessna down on Beaverhouse and taxied up to the
wooden dock at the ranger station.

"Scottie," I said, "give us the canister. We ought to

be able to shake enough dust off our stuff to fill at least a third of it."

Scottie didn't look hopeful, but he handed me the can and took off over the lake. The Bear and I lugged our gear to a little clearing with a view of the lake and a forest floor covered with pine needles. We pitched the tent, unrolled our sleeping bags, unpacked the box of food, and shook out our clothes. The dust of Tom's ashes was so fine we couldn't recover enough to fill a salt shaker.

That night after supper—chicken stew, the Bear's sourdough biscuits, and fresh blueberries in a Sierra cup—as we sat around the fire talking and drinking coffee, I took out a couple of White Owl cigars from the top pocket of my field jacket, and we lit up. It struck me that the solution to our problem was as close as the end of our cigars. I held up my cigar with a smile.

"You're not thinking what I'm thinking?" the Bear said.

He rummaged around in the tent and came back with the canister. We sat against a log and smoked the White Owls, knocking the ashes into the canister. The texture was too coarse, so I stirred the ashes with a birch twig till they were fine enough.

For the next two nights we had a ritual: cook supper, wash the dishes, make a pot of coffee, sit by the fire, smoke our White Owls, and fill Tom's ash can. Quetico had been kind to us: the sun was warm, the breeze was light, and the loons sang their mournful songs for Tom.

The last night we had a feast of steaks, fried pota-toes, a pot of beans, and the last slices from a loaf of homemade rye bread. After we had washed the dishes and poured the coffee, I reached for the last of the White Owls. The Bear held up his hand to stop me.

"I've been thinking," he said. "Maybe we're treating this ashes business a little too lightly. Suppose old Tom was a cigar smoker. He'd want something more than a White Owl."

The Bear reached into his shirt pocket and pulled out two silver cylinders of foil-wrapped Cuban cigars. They were Reas Coronas, full-bodied and easy-smok-ing. We unwrapped them, lit up, and puffed.

When the ashes were about an inch long, the Bear said, "How'd that go again, the funeral service?"

"From ashes to ashes and dust to dust," I said.

The Bear took another puff and dropped the ash in the can at his side.

LESSONS ON THE JOURNEY

This book was designed, composed, and
illustrated by Dennis Anderson.
The text was set on an Apple Macintosh
in Dante Monotype.

This book was produced by
Nodin Press, a division of Micawber's, Inc.
525 North Third Street
Minneapolis, MN 55401